SHADOW'S CONSPIRACY

SHADOW ISLAND SERIES: BOOK EIGHT

MARY STONE

LORI RHODES

MARY
STONE
PUBLISHING

This book is dedicated to the courageous men and women who, with unyielding spirit, step into the face of danger each day. We honor their strength, their commitment, and the light they bring to the darkest of shadows.

DESCRIPTION

Not every conspiracy is a theory.

When a man washes up onto Shadow Island, Sheriff Rebecca West has a moment of déjà vu. This isn't the first body the ocean spat out on one of her beaches, but it's the first one she's found alive.

Barely.

The brutal gunshot wounds to the victim's hand and the lower part of his face indicate he was shot offshore and dumped overboard, but there's no boat or perpetrator. Just a few cryptic clues before the victim becomes unresponsive.

At first glance, the investigation points to pirates or a drug deal gone bad. But as Rebecca delves deeper, she realizes that this is far more than an attempt on a low-level criminal's life. The case stretches out its tendrils, entangling the esteemed members of Shadow Island's Select Board, the sinister Yacht Club, and even her own sheriff's department.

And it could jeopardize everything.

Blackmail, power, and corruption collide as Rebecca resolves to clean the island up once and for all. Unless she dies trying.

From its puzzling beginning to the devastating conclusion, Shadow's Conspiracy—the eighth book in the Shadow Island Series by Mary Stone and Lori Rhodes—will make you realize that whatever you sweep under the rug always comes back to haunt you.

1

"Hail, Mary, full of grace, um, we beseech thee and...and..."

Dammit to hell.

Catechism had been too long ago, and Chester Able hadn't had much interest in praying since then. Now that he needed to, he couldn't remember the words, but that didn't stop him from trying.

"I beseech thee." His whispers were barely audible. "Help me get my stupid ass out of this situation and I swear I'll light a candle every day from now on. I'll even come in and confess my sins."

As a gunshot rang out below him, Chester desperately searched for a way out of his predicament. His feet lost traction on the polished upper deck of the yacht, and he bit his lip to stop himself from cursing.

He scrambled in an undignified crawl on his toes and forearms, trying to make himself as small as possible while he sneaked around to the boat's stern. The last thing he wanted was to be seen by the men with the guns.

The gunshot didn't bode well for one of his two companions. Chester was determined not to meet a similar fate.

Even though he was the only one currently on the second level, two staircases led up to the sundeck, where he cowered on the port side. The stupid, bright, moonlit sky would surely give him away if he left his hiding spot.

And the crazy son of a bitch on the control deck will find me easily enough if he just looks up.

Right now, the only thing telling Chester he was currently safe was the babbling voice of the one guy who hadn't been shot yet. But neither of them had the information their attackers were looking for.

Only Chester did.

Something large splashed into the water off the port side, and he flinched.

Shit!

One of his friends had just become fish food, but he dared not sneak a peek. Silently, he prayed for his companion's soul, but he was interrupted by an angry voice echoing off the water. It faded as another voice responded, whining and begging.

He had to get away while they were still talking.

The men with the guns had approached them using an inflatable raft. They'd rowed over from the island and boarded the yacht before anyone understood what was happening. Landon, who was now pleading for his life, had been the one tasked with keeping a lookout.

Dumbass left his post!

And now, these pirates were near the bow. Chester would have to climb down to get away. But if he did that, he ran the risk of being seen. And if he didn't lower himself slowly into the water, the splash he made would surely draw the attention he was desperate to avoid.

Chester figured God might be on his side in this matter.

Although things looked grim, his luck had held out when the men had fixated on one of his pals and not even bothered to search the boat for more crew. Now if only that luck, or divine intervention, would hold.

A ragged cry of pain from the main deck sent chills down his spine.

Chester pulled himself up to the railing and peeked over. The bright moonlight revealed there were no boats nearby to lend aid. And the distant shoreline of Shadow Island was dotted with lights from homes, its occupants winding down for the night, unaware of Chester's predicament.

Running without lights was normal for Chester's little group when they weren't partying, and it always made the trips more fun and mysterious. Unfortunately, that meant he couldn't see if any other boats—help—were close either.

The angriest man's intensity was growing as he shouted, and Landon continued begging for his life.

It was time to bail on this voyage.

Spinning in a circle, Chester made sure one last time that he was the only one on this level. His prayers had worked. The sundeck was only ever used for tanning, hooking up, or, as it was tonight, standing lookout.

Fat lot of good that did.

This deck was smaller, so he could make out the tops of the heads of the five menacing intruders gathered at the bow.

Something pale caught his eye, and he gulped. Down in the water, the white shirt of his dead colleague was turning a dark pink as saltwater dispersed the blood flooding out of the fist-sized exit hole in his upper back.

Freddie always loved that shirt.

They'd blown Freddie's heart out.

Chester had watched enough action movies to know that was a terrible way to die.

He dropped in reflex as another explosion went off on the

deck below. Pained screams kept him huddled and his limbs trembling in terror.

No. No. No.

They were moving too fast. He had to get in position. Jumping from this height would be certain death. He needed to get to the main deck where he could ease into the water.

Clawing over to the ladder with shaky arms, he began lowering himself to the stern.

"Find the other one!"

Chester's foot slipped on a rung. He was "the other one." Had they known he was here all along?

His fingers clutched the top of the ladder, white-knuckled with terror, as he tried to hold himself in position. He locked his attention on the faint lights in the distance—the only signs of humanity in the world as the acrid smell of gunpowder on the briny breeze infiltrated his nose. Swimming had always been something he excelled at. He couldn't tell how far away those lights were, but that didn't stop him from telling himself he could make it.

There was no other choice. It was swim or die. And he didn't want to die.

These men were going to toss Landon's body anytime now. He had to get to the main deck so he could slip over the railing. It was only three feet to the water there, and he could ease himself in.

Trembling with fear, he continued his descent. His knees felt like rubber, and he briefly wondered where his sea legs had gone. But he knew his unsteadiness came from the presence of unwelcome visitors on his boat and not his years of seafaring.

Then three things happened at once.

A viselike grip clutched his ankle as he prepared to move to the next rung on the ladder.

The second body, Landon, splashed into the water behind him.

And Chester's hands slipped as fear and horror caused his body to convulse.

Too late, he tried to grab back onto the rails, but he was dragged down and slammed onto the deck. Far too late, he understood that he should've jumped when the attack first started. It would've been better to fall into the ocean and worry about being shot than be at the mercy of these men.

He twisted reflexively as the back of his head bounced off the metal railing on the first deck. Stars washed across his vision. Blinding pain reverberated through his skull, rattling his teeth. His body went limp from shock.

Then he crumpled sideways into a pretzel, his ankle still held by one of the invaders. He was face down on the wooden planking, trying to figure out how to untangle himself. From a knot growing on the back of his head, warm blood trickled down his neck.

"If you're going to try to hide," the man holding his ankle barked as a lightning bolt of pain shot through Chester's leg, "you shouldn't be bumbling around above our heads."

As his leg was brutally slammed into the railing, Chester miraculously found his voice. "Help! Someone, help!"

Sinister chuckles enveloped him. He looked, really looked, at the man holding his ankle.

He was dark-haired with a jagged scar across his forehead, and he was casually tapping the barrel of a huge, shiny handgun against Chester's shin. He dropped Chester's leg and moved closer to his catch, leaving red-tinged footprints on the deck.

Chester swallowed thickly. His friends' blood.

"Go ahead. Scream your head off." Flinging his arms wide, the man threw back his head and unleashed a bestial roar, which faded into laughter. He leaned over Chester, smiling.

Rancid breath assaulted Chester's nose and brought bile to his throat. Or maybe it was the concussion he most definitely had. Fear trickled down his leg in a hot, wet line. If he hadn't been so afraid for his life, he would've been horribly embarrassed.

"No one cares if you scream. There's nobody around to hear it. But you can keep making a fool of yourself if you want." The pirate gestured down at Chester's wet groin with the pistol, making him tense up even more. "So let's get to business. You know what I want. You and your little friends have stepped into something much too big for you. I need the names of your suppliers."

Chester clamped his lips, realizing the tenuous situation he was in. If he gave his suppliers' names, he was dead. If he didn't, he was dead.

Rock. Hard place. Me right in the middle.

The man with the scar tilted his head. His eyes reminded Chester of a snake's.

"They didn't answer my questions either. Look what happened."

"I don't know anything," Chester blubbered, lying. "I only worked for those other two." Pulling himself up to his feet, he nearly fell as his ankle twinged.

"Oh, don't say that." The gunman clicked his tongue and shook his head sadly. "If you don't know anything," the gun rose to point at Chester's throat, "then I have no reason to keep you alive."

Chester's full attention was centered on the yawning barrel pointed at him. He swore he could see down its interior. Staring at the bullet that would end his life.

Damn moonlight!

He gulped, straightening reflexively. "I can't tell you what I don't know."

"Well, then." The man raised his gun higher.

Making the sign of the cross and with a final kiss to his knuckle, Chester finished his prayer.

If the man said anything else, Chester didn't hear. The gun spoke so loudly, it erased every other sound.

WARMTH on his back and a wet snuffling sound in his ear roused Chester. His entire body screamed in pain. He tried to open his eyes, but fierce golden rays stabbed into them. Clenching them shut, he tried to figure out what had happened.

I must be dead.

The warm, soft sand at his back, the silky touch on his cheek, and the figure he couldn't see. It all pointed to one thing.

He was before the gates of Heaven. Judgment Day was upon him, like his mom had always warned. And he knew he would be found lacking. Tears filled his eyes.

"I'm sorry."

The words were barely audible. His mouth was full of grit, and his throat was tight and parched. He tried to lick his lips, but his jaw refused to unhinge. Heaven tasted like…salt.

Chester told himself salt was a cleansing agent, wiping his sins away, choking him with redemption. He coughed to clear his throat. He had to tell someone what had happened.

"Two more." His voice sounded raw. Working his jaw hurt.

"What?" A shadow formed over him. It was the dark silhouette of a giant woman. An angel? "Two more what? Brody, down!"

The angel was asking him questions. This had to be a test to show how true his repentance was. He struggled to reach into his pocket. His right hand didn't work. "Password. Fallen. There're two more. Find them."

Somewhere out there were the bodies of his friends. Maybe they had done bad things, but they were good guys. They deserved better than to become food for the fish. Even criminals deserved last rites.

Tears burned his eyes as he struggled to stare up at the angel through the golden haze surrounding his face. "Save them."

"I will. And I'll get you help. It'll be okay."

The angel continued to talk to him, but he could no longer hear her. His regrets addressed, Chester finally let go. Warm air and fur bathed his face. It felt like Heaven.

"Brody, no!"

His last thought was that Heaven tasted like salt...but smelled like wet dog.

2

Sheriff Rebecca West hopped out of her Explorer. With the word *Sheriff* emblazoned in large letters down the SUV's side doors, it was never a problem finding parking, especially at the Shadow Island Community Health Center.

Because of her athletic build and shoulder-length blond hair, people tended to not believe she could be in law enforcement at all, let alone an ex-FBI special agent. They could never say why, but Rebecca was certain they expected a giant Amazonian warrior or something. The shiny Explorer parked in the designated police parking space did help with that.

Not having an official uniform still...did not.

She'd gotten the call to come in early when they'd found a man on the shore of Beaman Beach. Not the best way to start a morning. Especially one that'd begun with a leisurely breakfast on her back deck with Ryker Sawyer after waking up in his arms once again.

Rebecca hurried in through the front doors, heading straight for the nurses' station around the corner in the center of the building. Over the last month, she'd spent an awful lot of time in this facility.

With her badge pulled, Rebecca walked up to the desk. She sighed when she recognized the back of the nurse. It was easy to tell who it was by the inverted bob and shaved back and sides. "Don't you ever get a day off?"

Missy turned, raised her eyebrows, and laughed. "I could say the same thing about you." She finished filing her papers and slid them into one of the cubbies underneath the counter. "Can I assume that our newest patient is what brought you in today?"

Rebecca put her badge away. Missy knew who she was. There was no need to go flashing her brass.

The nurse came over and grimaced.

Her bleak expression made Rebecca sigh. "Don't tell me he died on the way in."

"Nope. I'm not on his case. But he's not looking too good." There was a hint of sadness in Missy's honey-brown eyes. The sign of a medical professional who'd seen too much death and now expected it.

"I was told he was talking."

"Was. Past tense." Missy pulled a chair out and sank into it with a relieved sigh before rotating her shoulders. "They ventilated him shortly after he came in. I'm sorry, I don't know anything more right now. They're still working on him. We've arranged emergency transport. He needs to get to Coastal Ridge ASAP."

"Boss?"

Rebecca twisted to look down the hallway. Senior Deputy Hoyt Frost waved as he headed over from the patient rooms.

"Thought I heard your voice." With his lanky frame and long legs, he covered ground quickly.

"I thought you'd still be at the scene. You left Darian on the beach?"

He tilted his head with a hint of a smile. "He insisted. Said he had 'something to deal with.'"

Rebecca and her deputy, Darian Hudson, once had a heart-to-heart a month ago while a hurricane was ravaging the island. The "something to deal with" message made them aware the other person was dealing with their PTSD and needed some space. It kept the questions to a minimum. And the whole code had been facilitated by Hoyt in a protective act for his friend and colleague. Now Rebecca was a part of that too.

But this was the first time Rebecca had ever heard their code phrase used that way. Her trigger was the smell of engine oil. Darian's was sand getting in his boots, which was why they didn't send him to the beach unless it couldn't be helped. She couldn't stop her face from registering surprise as she raised an eyebrow.

Darian's trauma was no one else's business. As his boss, she was relieved he could handle the scene despite his triggers. As his friend, she was happy to think that he might one day get to enjoy a day at the beach with his wife and baby. Everyone knew Lilian wanted to share with her family her love for the fun and creativity of playing in the sand.

Hoyt shook his head, holding up a large plastic bag. "I came in with the victim. He kept talking about 'two more' and 'fallen' before he stopped breathing. EMTs had to bag him after that. I thought we'd lost him before we even rolled him through the entrance."

Rebecca finally got a peek at what was in the plastic bag. "Are those his clothes?"

"Yup. They had to cut them off. So they're ours now. He won't be needing them when they transfer him to the mainland."

"Get them in paper bags so they can dry out and not

mold. It'll destroy the blood evidence if it stays wet. There are a couple paper bags in the Explorer."

"Will do."

Rebecca indicated the hallway, which led to their victim. "Could you tell what was wrong with him? Was he attacked, or was this an accident?"

"Not sure yet. He's got a nasty gash on the back of his head, doc says a concussion to go with it, was half drowned, and his hand was damn near destroyed. And the lower part of his face. Possibly from a gunshot. Though the doctor isn't ruling out a horrible fall. He did keep saying 'fallen' after all. The hand and jaw were already wrapped by the time I got on scene, so I didn't see the injuries themselves."

"He'd have to be pretty damn high up to have sustained those kinds of injuries from a fall. How would he even get that high? It's not like there're cliffs around here or anything."

"Falling out of a fast-moving boat could do it, if you hit a few things on the way down. I'm not sure what we're working with here. We'll need to wait for the doctor to let us know."

"Well, we need to find out as soon as possible if there are two more people out there. What do we know about the guy?"

Hoyt hefted the bag. "Thought I felt a wallet in the pocket. We can start there."

"You two can use the desk over here." Missy pointed to her left at the empty space behind the counter. "Just don't get the papers wet. Transport should be here soon, so I need to take care of some paperwork for the transfer."

"Thanks, Missy." Hoyt walked around the counter, and Rebecca joined him. They pulled on gloves, not only to protect the evidence but because there were splashes of diluted blood covering every piece of soaked clothing. The bag was the simple drawstring kind the hospital handed out to put personal items in. Hoyt felt along the sides 'til he found what he wanted and moved it to the top.

"Here we go." The wallet he pulled out was a basic leather bifold, nothing unique about it except it was stored in a resealable sandwich bag. "I guess he knew there could be a chance of it getting wet."

Hoyt flipped the wallet open. "Chester Able of Baltimore, Maryland. That's our guy in there." He tilted the wallet to show her the ID window.

Inside, she found a driver's license photo of a man with dirty-blond hair, hazel eyes, and a nose that had clearly been broken a few times. The date of birth on his license indicated he was just shy of his fortieth birthday.

"Anything else that might tell us what he was doing down here?"

Hoyt continued flipping through the wallet. "A couple of credit cards and a condom that looks like it could be old enough to have its own kids by now, but that's about it. No receipts or anything like that. Not even a parking stub."

An elderly woman in a long white coat that marked her as a doctor briskly approached and reached over the counter. She'd clearly come from something messy, as she still had on a thin hairnet that nearly hid her cornrows.

Missy handed her a bottle of hand sanitizer without looking up from her work.

"Dr. Jane Olson, this is Sheriff West. West, this is Dr. Olson," Hoyt said. "She's on Chester's case."

"Chester? So you did get a name?" Dr. Olson had to rise onto her toes to peek over the counter in the effort to view her patient's ID as she worked the sanitizer over her hands.

"Chester Able, thirty-nine, one hundred and eighty pounds." Rebecca read off the information as she pulled out her notepad. "Is he able to give a victim statement?"

"Sadly, no. We got him breathing on his own again, but he's still unconscious. There's a large gash on the back of his head. He has a pretty jagged laceration along his jawline, which I suspect is broken. I believe there's a bullet lodged in there. He'll need x-rays and a CT scan, but we needed to get him stable first. I suspect he's got a couple fractures. He's lost a lot of blood. The wound to his hand barely missed the radial artery, and water can prevent clotting. Not to mention open water and an open wound are a bad combination. Lots of microbes." She waved her hand at the bag of clothes. "That's all yours, though. GSW means it's criminal."

"That rules out our boating accident theory. Where was he shot?"

Dr. Olson picked up a clipboard and flipped through the papers. "Gunshot wound to the wrist. His hand was probably near his face, trying to deflect. A pretty typical defensive posture."

Rebecca held her hand up in front of herself. "Like this?"

The doctor nodded and replicated the gesture, tapping the bone below her wrist on the little-finger side. "Went straight through the ulna, shattering it, and lodged in his mandible. I've already consulted with a surgeon at Coastal Ridge, because even though I've managed to stabilize the man, we need to get him to the mainland stat so he can undergo surgery. Hopefully, the surgeon can save his hand. They should be able to remove the bullet in his jaw cleanly. They can collect it for ballistics."

Rebecca's pen blazed over her notepad to keep up with Dr. Olson's rapid-fire report.

Dr. Olson checked the clock on the wall before glancing at the patient's chart again. "Able also sustained a nasty fracture to his ankle. The folks at Coastal Ridge will need to get images of that too. We've immobilized it for now, but it's pretty mangled."

"Any thoughts on how he might've sustained that injury?"

Dr. Olson gave one shake of her head. "It doesn't appear to have external lacerations like it would if he caught it on something. But there are a number of other ways he could have injured it. Maybe he hit it on something while swimming. I'd hate to speculate further."

"Thanks." Rebecca glanced down at Able's bag of soaked clothes.

"The EMTs said he was talking about two more?" Dr. Olson adjusted the stethoscope around her neck.

Rebecca nodded. "That's what it sounds like."

"Then we'll make sure we're ready for them. And can you let us know as soon as you find next of kin? And do that as soon as possible." Dr. Olson was too experienced to let her expression give anything away, but Rebecca knew what she meant.

Chester wasn't doing well, and they would likely need next of kin on hand to make medical decisions for him. Or funeral arrangements.

"Good thing we've got this, then." Hoyt worked up another resealable bag—this one containing a cell phone carefully wrapped inside—from within the scraps of clothing. "We can check his contacts."

Screeching tires out front of the Community Health Center put everyone on high alert.

The ER doors slid open and two EMTs rushed through. The chestnut-brown hair of the woman was secured in a tight bun at the back of her head. Catching the doctor's eye, she immediately closed the space between them. Her ID badge read Sandra Baker. Rebecca remembered her from the mermaid case during the hurricane.

"We're here for the critical patient."

Dr. Olson nodded to Nurse Missy, who was all business now. Handing a clipboard to the paramedic, she nodded at

Kendric Hayes, the other EMT, as he joined his partner. "Patient's name is Chester Able, age thirty-nine. GSW to the wrist. Intubated on arrival. Significant blood loss and suspected skull fracture. He's been stabilized and is ready for transport."

Baker returned the signed transfer papers to Nurse Missy with a curt nod before following her partner and the nurse down the hallway.

A moment later, Hoyt and Rebecca stepped out of the way as the paramedics rushed from Chester's room and hustled their patient lying on a gurney out the doors and into the back of the waiting ambulance.

Rebecca hoped Chester survived the trip. After all, dead men couldn't tell tales.

3

R ebecca was careful to make sure the evidence bags she was carrying didn't snag on the door to the sheriff's station.

"Sorry I had to call you in so early." Melody Jenkins was still sitting at the dispatch desk. Her tan was dark and went well with her wavy auburn hair. Every time Rebecca saw her, she felt a pang of jealousy, thinking about how much time she must spend at the beach. Her glowing, sun-kissed look was, no doubt, thanks to working nights.

"No worries. Split shifts like today's always run the risk of an early call-in or late departure. There's no rest for the wicked and even less for those who pursue them." Rebecca swung the bags ahead of her, then twisted so the fob on her keys would unlock the half door that led into the offices. "Any word from the beach?"

"Not a peep. Need me to call over there?"

"No. I'm sure Darian will call if he needs anything. Viviane isn't in yet?"

Melody shook her head, sending the gentle waves of her hair bouncing. "She texted me saying her class was running a bit late. It's all good, though." She glanced up at the clock on the wall. "Viviane also said she'll work ten hours once she gets back to cover. Then I'll work my normal shift, dinner to midnight, until the answering service takes over, if that's okay with you."

"That's fine." The distinctive sound of claws on tile stole Rebecca's attention as a golden flurry came running up to her. "Brody! What are you doing here, boy?" Setting the evidence bags on the counter, she bent over to ruffle her neighbor's golden retriever.

"Sorry, Rebecca." Kelly Hunt, Brody's mom and the first casual friend Rebecca had made after moving to Shadow Island, came around the wall from the bullpen. She'd grown up in Florida but moved to the island several years ago. "He got away from me again. I lost his leash somewhere."

"I'm glad you found him. Did someone turn him in here?" Rebecca got a good look at Kelly's face and saw worry and anxiety etched in deep lines.

The brows over Kelly's slender nose pulled downward in a frown. "No. Well, yes. Well, we're here to give our statement." She pointed at her dog, who was now happily turning circles between the two women. "We're the ones who found that poor man this morning. Mel said we should wait back here, so I just let Brody wander around a bit. He didn't get into anything important, though. I swear."

"Oh, Kelly, I'm so sorry. Why don't you follow me back to my office so I can set this stuff down? Then I'll take your statement."

Hooking her fingers through Brody's collar, Kelly followed Rebecca back to her office with her dog in tow.

"Have a seat. Make yourself comfortable." Rebecca set the bags on her desk and opened a drawer to pull out a recorder. "I'm going to record this so it can all be transcribed later. Are you okay with that?" She laughed out loud when she saw

Kelly sitting in the chair closest to the door and Brody turning circles in the other chair before flopping down.

Seeing where she was looking, Kelly turned and sighed. Her dog's muzzle rested on the arm of the chair closest to her, and he was staring at her with loving eyes. "Oh, Brody, you're really in a mood today, aren't you? I'm sorry, Rebecca. Sheriff. Sorry."

"He's fine. I'm sure he's just reacting to how you're feeling. Are you okay?" Rebecca waved her hand at Brody, but he wasn't paying her a bit of attention. "Because he doesn't seem to think so."

"I'm fine. I mean, well…" Kelly looked at her dog, whose tail wagged a tiny bit, and stroked his head. "I'm not. He's right. I'm not. That man. Oh, god, Rebecca, it was so awful. His skin was all swollen and his hand was completely mangled. I'm not sure what happened to his head, but it didn't look right. It was awful." Her hand shook, and Brody pulled himself up higher in the seat so he could scoot closer.

After turning on the recorder and stating who was present, Rebecca began asking Kelly the necessary questions. "Why don't you start at the beginning? What were you doing on Beaman Beach this morning? You know I know, but this is for your statement."

"I was taking Brody for our morning walk. You know he likes to greet everyone he sees. So when he's particularly rambunctious, like he was this morning, we head up to Beaman. It's less crowded there. When we got close to the open stretch of sand, he slipped his collar and took off. Now that I'm thinking about it, maybe he saw or smelled that man and that was why he got free. He was just lying there. I wasn't sure what it was at first, and I was running, trying to catch up with Brody."

"Where exactly was that?"

"Just south of the three dunes where the coast starts to

curve to the west again. You know the place? The man was in the sand, barely below the high tide line. And he wasn't moving." Kelly's fingers stilled in Brody's long golden fur. "I thought he was dead. I started praying right off the bat as I ran up. I wanted to help him, but I was so scared. I was scared he might be dead, and even more scared he was dying." With guilty eyes, she stared at Rebecca.

"I get that. I do. You didn't want to see him die or feel helpless."

Kelly nodded and went back to petting her dog.

"Then he started talking. It was hard to hear him. Brody was at his head, sniffing him. Then he tried to lift his head as he opened his eyes. He was on his back. There was something…wrong with the back of his head. I'm not sure how to describe it, and I was afraid to touch him. But his skull was, like, sunken, I guess. His arms were at weird angles to his body. I didn't even notice his right hand at first. I came up to him from his left side." Her eyes brimmed with tears. "He seemed so sad. And he kept mumbling the same words."

"What was he saying?"

"Two more. Fallen. Password." Kelly bit her lips and shook her head. "I think. That was all I could make out. And I didn't know what to do. I saw the blood and his head looked wrong too. I was scared I would hurt him if I moved him, so I just left him lying there the whole time while I called 911."

Rebecca slid a box of tissues across her desk. "That was the right thing to do. We've since learned he has a severe head injury. It was good that you didn't move him. Don't blame yourself for leaving him like that. You very well could've saved his life by leaving him alone. Calling for help was the right thing to do."

"I felt so helpless. I couldn't even hold his hand. To let him know he wasn't alone. Brody lay down by his head." She sniffled and glanced at her dog, who was happily getting his ear scratched now. "He seemed to know what to do, so I just sat with them and prayed while we waited. And I kept talking to him. I don't know if he heard me or not...he didn't respond. I kept telling him it was going to be okay, and help was on the way."

"Was there anyone else around?"

Kelly shook her head, and her wavy hair swayed. "No one. There's usually not anyone there at that time, and no houses nearby. I'd already called for help. But I did keep looking around. I don't know why. Just hoping someone else would show up. So, you know, we wouldn't be alone."

Rebecca's heart squeezed for her friend. "That's understandable."

She let out a self-deprecating laugh. "I was supposed to be with him so he wasn't alone, but I wanted someone else there for me so I didn't feel alone. Selfish."

"It wasn't selfish at all. That was reasonable and responsible. The more people there, the more likely he would get the help he needed."

Kelly finally took the tissue and dabbed at her eyes.

"I felt so alone out there."

Kelly's mind had been emotionally hijacked, and Rebecca needed her to think more rationally. Questions were the best way to shift a person's brain to the logical side, so she peppered her with a couple. "Can you remember if you saw any boats on the water? Tracks in the sand?"

Kelly blinked as she considered the questions, her trembling easing a bit. "Nothing. Just Brody's. Not even the man's. They were probably washed away when the tide went out."

"Or maybe a friendly current brought in our Mr. Able. But there were no boats nearby?"

"Not even in the shipping lanes, as far as I could see. Just me, him, Brody, and the morning sun."

Rebecca wrote a few notes to check when high tide

started and ended. "Okay, back to him. When did he start talking?"

"He was talking when I walked up. To Brody, I think. He said, 'Two more.' I asked him, 'Two more what?' Then he moved. Reaching for his leg."

"Did he answer you?"

Kelly shook her head. "No, but that's when he said 'password' and 'fallen.'" Her eyes widened slightly, and she sniffled. "No, he did say something else. He asked me to save them. 'Find them and save them.' That's when I looked around. To check if there were more people out there. But I didn't see anyone at all."

"You said he reached for his leg?" Rebecca glanced at the bags of evidence again, which held his clothes.

"Yeah, I think he was reaching for his pocket. The lower one. He was wiggling his fingers at it. He looked so desperate. I think he wanted something, but I was too afraid to touch him." She shrugged and shifted in her seat. Brody's eyes popped open as he checked on her.

"Did you notice anything else unusual out there today? Anything at all? Think back to when you started your walk all the way up until when my men arrived on the scene."

Kelly closed her eyes for a moment and shook her head. "Everything was normal. Quiet and still. No one else around. Nothing interesting in the sand either. A good start to the morning. When you want to get up and move but not have to think too much, you know?"

"I know." And Rebecca did know. She also liked to get her exercises in first thing in the morning before she was awake enough to truly feel it. It'd only been a few months since she'd had her shoulder surgery, so she still had to do painful stretching and strengthening exercises every day—otherwise it would stiffen up and heal improperly.

"I'm sorry I haven't been more helpful."

"Oh, no, you've been a great help. You saved that man's life. You and Brody, of course." It was never a bad thing to give a dog a bit of extra credit in Rebecca's book, and this time, she was certain it was true. Kelly didn't always walk that far north. If Brody hadn't gotten loose and run to Chester Able, there was nothing to say he wouldn't have been left lying there for the rest of the morning.

Kelly's weak smile, a tip to her natural positivity, kept slipping off her face. "You're just saying that to be nice to me."

Rebecca shook her head and reached for the evidence bags. "Not at all." She pulled a set of gloves from the box she kept in her drawer and slipped them on before pulling out the bagged phone.

"What were the words he told you?" Rebecca pressed the button on the side and saw that the phone was locked but working. She unwrapped one of the plastic bags around it.

"Two more. Password. Fallen. Find them."

Rebecca typed on the keypad through the remaining bag and the phone unlocked. "His password was *fallen*." She lifted her gaze to Kelly. "Without you, we wouldn't have known that." She searched for the settings and changed the security to turn off the lock screen. "Now we can find where he was and maybe even find the two others he talked about."

Kelly mouthed *oh* and, this time, her smile was genuine. "I guess I was helpful after all."

"You were. Why don't you go home now before I slap a badge on your shirt and recruit you to the team?"

Kelly laughed, and the tightness in Rebecca's chest eased a little more. "No, thank you. If I never see anything like that again, it'll be too soon."

"Do you want a ride back? I can drop you off."

"No." Kelly waved her off and stood. "I'd rather walk home. I need time to think."

"I know it isn't far, but are you sure?"

"I'm sure." Brody jumped down to join her by the door. "He could use a bit more exercise after all the excitement today anyway. Isn't that right, my good boy?"

Brody stared up at her with all the devotion only a well-loved dog could express and wagged his tail.

Rebecca stood, too, and joined her at the door. "Let me walk you out then. You've been a big help."

Brody, sensing it was time to leave, trotted out the door and toward the exit, the two women walking behind him.

"Will you let me know how that man is doing? Later. When you can?" Kelly's voice was shaky again, making Rebecca concerned for her.

"I will. As soon as I can. Are you sure you're okay to walk home?"

Viviane was behind the dispatch desk and settling into work, tucking her headset into her hair. She offered both women a brief wave.

"I'll be fine. Just need some air." She gestured to the warm, sunny day on the other side of the glass door. Brody didn't wait for anyone else and jumped over the half door into the lobby. Kelly laughed. "And I think somebody needs a potty break too."

Rebecca smiled at the dog's antics. "I'll call you later to make sure you got home safe."

"Sounds good. Bye, Rebecca, Viviane."

"Bye." Viviane watched her leave before turning her concerned dark eyes toward Rebecca. "Is she okay?"

"Probably not. But she will be if Chester Able pulls through." Rebecca sighed and leaned against the dispatch desk next to Viviane. "You think you're ready to do some investigative work?"

Viviane sat up straight in her chair, beaming. "Yeah, Boss! What you got?"

Rebecca held the wrapped phone out. "This is Chester's phone. He tried to hand it to Kelly when she found him and told her the password so she could 'find two more and save them.' That clears us to use it. Victim's consent."

Viviane nodded, but Rebecca noticed her write down *victim's consent* and knew she'd look it up when she had a chance.

"Go through it and track down everything you can, including any locations, contacts, phone numbers he's called, and any more information you can dig up."

Viviane started to reach for the bag then froze. She opened a drawer and pulled out gloves from a sealed package. "On it. You going to watch over my shoulder, or…?"

"No, I think you've got this. I also need you to dust the phone for fingerprints. Do you remember how to do that from your classes?"

"Sure do." The giant smile on Viviane's face stood in contrast to the severity of the situation, but Rebecca understood her friend's pride.

"I'm leaving to check in with Hudson at the crime scene and let him know what we've learned."

"I'll have this all done before you get back, Boss."

Rebecca stripped off her gloves and rested her hand on Viviane's arm. "I don't want it fast, Vi. I want it thorough. Can you also ask forensics to swing by and pick up the bags from my office?"

Viviane's lips tightened, then she broke into another grin. There was no keeping this woman down. "I can do both."

"Great." Rebecca pulled her keys from her pocket, tossing her gloves in the garbage can. "I'm heading out to see if I can find our *two more.*"

4

_____

"Okay, gentlemen, what do we have?" Rebecca had trudged through the hot sand at Beaman Beach to where her senior deputy was standing next to their consultant. Greg Abner was long retired from the force but would work a few hours with the department when they needed extra hands or another set of eyes.

During an honest moment in the midst of a hurricane's onslaught, he'd shared his feelings about Deputy Trent Locke. Rebecca had learned Locke was hired in a rush to replace Greg since he wanted to retire. But then Greg had returned almost as quickly when he'd assessed that the new hire didn't know what he was doing.

But Rebecca's opinion of Deputy Locke was beginning to change, and she suspected the other deputies were coming around as well. After her trip through the swamp with Locke and their encounter with a leech-covered killer, she believed the deputy simply needed better training and less influence from his "friends" in the Yacht Club. But properly training him would take time, and that was something Rebecca never seemed to have enough of.

Today, Greg was spending his Saturday searching the beach. As a lifelong resident of the island, he knew it all like the back of his age-spotted hand and had forgotten more things about boats, fishing, and sailing than she'd ever learned. The deep wrinkles around his eyes showed how often he squinted against the sun. Lately, most of that was done from the bench on his fishing boat. Rebecca hoped his presence on this case would make a big difference.

"Without any reports of boating accidents, we sent all the civvy volunteers home. Forensics still isn't here." Hoyt waved his arm over the fairly small area that'd been taped off with crime scene markers. "There won't be a lot for them to collect in this tiny spot."

"Did we find anything else?" Locke and Darian paced the beach in both directions. They were swiveling their heads back and forth as they searched for any more survivors, bodies, evidence, or a secondary site.

"*Nada.*" Greg shook his head. "There's not much to see either. The three dunes there, another set on the north side... we've checked all those and didn't find anyone. There's no one out there except the sunbathers and us."

"That's on our side of things, though." Rebecca waved her finger at the water. "What about out there?"

"Well, there're the shipping lanes...usual boat traffic now that it's later in the day. Little Quell Island looks empty. And there's no sign of any recent wrecks or disabled boats." Greg did a slow turn in place. "Nothing out of the ordinary here."

"Our victim said something about falling," Hoyt reminded her.

"Yeah, about that. Turns out *fallen* was the password for his phone. He was trying to give it to Kelly Hunt so she could open it. He also asked us to find the other two who are allegedly missing. That's consent to search, so I handed it off to Viviane, and she's going to track down contacts and look through it while I'm out here. I even tasked her with dusting for prints."

Greg grunted. "Our girl is growing up. I still remember when she'd come in and hide under the counter to draw. It's hard to believe she's an adult now. I still keep a stash of hot cocoa mix in my desk for her." He grinned, but it quickly changed to a frown when he met Rebecca's questioning gaze. "What?"

"She still drinks it. I've seen her add it to her shakes too." Rebecca chuckled. "I didn't know you were her supplier, and I never figured out where she was getting it from."

His grin came back stronger than before, with a paternal gleam to it. "Well, Hudson has some too. For emergencies."

Recalling the case from June, when she'd grabbed some hot cocoa for three young girls on their way to the hospital after being saved from a trafficking ring, Rebecca beamed with pride that she got to work with such caring folks. They were more like family than coworkers. "That's good thinking. I like that."

"Okay, Boss, so what are we going to do next?" Hoyt pointed down the beach to where Darian was walking back after covering his search area. He was lifting each foot carefully and keeping to the still-wet sand—avoiding the loose stuff that could get into his boots—but he was facing his fears, nonetheless, and Rebecca was proud of him.

"If our beaches are clear, then we need to search farther out. I'm going to call Lettinger and ask if she's found our missing two. She's got boats too. We can use them to search the waters and even do a recon of Little Quell Island. There's not much more we can do about them until then, though."

"Time to go back to the office and start doing some desk work?" Greg arched one eyebrow at her.

"For us, yeah. We'll check into Chester. Can you talk to your fishing buddies and find out if they've seen anything?"

"Yeah, sure. It's a nice day out, but I won't say no to sitting down in the air-conditioning either." Greg waved his arm at the gentle waves. "Will Lettinger be able to set up a drag?"

"I'll contact the local PDs on the mainland around us first. But, yeah, we might need to do that too." She stared at the water, knowing how well it could hide any number of secrets. "Something's out there. I'll leave finding the other two to Agent Lettinger and the state police while we focus on figuring out what happened to our guy."

"You know what really bothers me, though?" Hoyt took his hat off long enough to push his hair back.

"What is it?" Rebecca turned to where he was staring and spotted Locke walking back empty-handed as well.

"If he came from the water, where's the boat he was on? And who shot him?" He turned his gaze back to her. "Pirates aren't unheard of in this area, but they're a lot worse than anything we've had to deal with before."

Greg pursed his lips like he was about to spit but then glanced at Rebecca and swallowed. "If we're dealing with pirates, this is gonna get real messy, real fast."

5

"You think Hudson's going to be okay out there?" Rebecca asked as they walked into the station together.

"He'll be fine." Hoyt gave Viviane a nod. "That counting trick he does keeps him pretty settled. And you know Army guys. They're always wanting to push themselves. And he's got a damn good reason to work on it. Something about exposure therapy, he said."

Rebecca shuddered at the thought. Exposure therapy meant constantly being around whatever a person was afraid of, or what triggered their PTSD. She'd known it was a possible treatment but had never been able to stomach the idea of doing that herself.

"He's a stronger person than me. I wish him all the luck."

"Stronger than most people I know too."

Viviane waved her over, holding a stack of papers.

Rebecca opened the half door for herself and Hoyt and moved over so she could see what their dispatcher had managed to find while they'd been out. "What've you got, Vi?"

"First off, I ran a background check on Chester Able. That's most of this stack." She waved the sheets of paper to show how many there were. "Most of these are drug related. Buying, selling, possession, possession with intent to distribute, along with random thefts and firearm possessions."

"Any grand theft or auto theft?" Hoyt leaned in to read over her shoulder.

Viviane shook her head. "Nothing that big. Mostly small stuff. Almost all of it when he was younger too. Oh, and one charge that reads like he got into a fistfight with an older teen and got caught."

"Could've been a gang initiation. Check for known associates that have links to gangs as well." Rebecca took the top page and read it over, searching for any aliases, but there were none.

"I can do that. But first, you might want to see this." Viviane pulled a few papers from the bottom of the stack. "The phone he had on him when he washed ashore is a burner. Bought a month ago. I called the data provider to check the hours it's been used."

"Considering how this case seems to be heading, I'm not all that surprised." If Chester was involved with pirates or drug dealers, that made a lot of sense. Pirates tended to target those they knew had lots of money and weren't likely to call the authorities. Drug runners would make damn good targets. Or this could've been a drug deal gone bad.

There were a lot of options to explore now.

"What else did you find?"

"After that, I checked his contacts and thought this one was pretty interesting." It was obvious she'd printed out the entire call log. She tapped a number, which she'd highlighted to show how many times it'd been called.

Rebecca read the area code. "Isn't that local?"

"It is. And you'll never believe whose it is." Viviane was nearly vibrating with excitement. "It's the landline at the residence of Mitchell Longfellow."

That name sounded familiar, and once she remembered where she knew it from, Rebecca gaped at Viviane. Luckily, Hoyt was as shocked as she was.

Viviane nodded sagely. "Yes, Select Board member and treasurer Mitchell Longfellow."

"Keep this under your hat, Viviane," Hoyt warned, taking the papers from her.

Rebecca looked pointedly at the door. "Let's take this to my office."

Viviane mimed zipping her lips and throwing away a key. "Mum's the word on that. Also, while you were out, I went ahead and signed for a package. Looks like the computer you ordered is here. I already called the folks at High Tide Tech Solutions too. They'll be here shortly to get everything set up."

Rebecca spotted the stack of boxes for the desktop she'd ordered to replace the old one at the spare desk in the bullpen. That one had been stripped for parts and left bare for longer than she'd been working there.

"That's good. Buzz me when they get here. And Vi, since you've proven so adept at multitasking, I have another favor. Can you please order me a proper uniform and a set of business cards? I think our witnesses are tired of me handing them used gum wrappers with my phone number scrawled across the inside."

Viviane gave a little salute.

Winking at her friend, Rebecca waved for Hoyt to follow her and headed for her office with all the information Viviane had dug up.

Hoyt flopped down in his regular chair then looked around as a puff of golden fur drifted up around him.

That nearly made Rebecca laugh, but then she remembered the anthill they'd just kicked over, and she shut the door to her office.

"Why the hell is a drug dealer calling a member of the Select Board?" Though Hoyt sounded calm, his hand shook as he picked dog hair off his uniform.

"Don't forget, Longfellow probably has links to the Yacht Club. He works and plays with members." Rebecca threw herself down into her seat and stared at the evidence piled up on her desk.

"So they're into dealing drugs now? I don't know. How do you want to handle this?" Hoyt leaned forward, resting his forearms on his knees.

Rebecca studied the call log Viviane had printed. "We've got to question him. That's for sure. Ole Mitch was the last person Chester called before he washed up on our shores. For all we know, he could've been planning a meeting with the man."

"You know, there's nothing to say Chester was far out in the water. He could've been attacked on the beach."

"That's possible. But we found nothing there. No footprints. No blood trails or signs of a struggle on scene. We'll see what forensics gets, but there was nothing showing anyone except Kelly and Brody had been on the beach. You were there first. Did you see anything?"

Lifting his hat, Hoyt pushed his hair back, a gesture that told her he was giving himself time to think. "No. No cars, no tracks. That far north from town, there're no parking lots with security cameras to check either. Just a hike from the road to the dunes. And his feet pointed toward the water with no marks around him. Like he'd been dumped there by a wave and not a person."

Rebecca rubbed her forehead. That was what she'd expected, and feared, considering Chester wasn't even from

Virginia. Still, she could request a warrant to get his financial information to see if he'd rented a car or even gotten a room on the island. It was half past noon on a Saturday. Judge Neumeyer wouldn't appreciate having his weekend interrupted, but he was her best option.

There was still one more lead to chase down. "Do you have a good relationship with Mitchell Longfellow?"

"I wouldn't call it *good*." Now he swiped at the stubborn golden fur on his slacks. "But we're not adversarial."

"Like I am with basically everyone on the board now." As much as Rebecca didn't want to care about the politics of the town, sheriff was still an elected position. Of course, that didn't stop certain members of the Select Board from behaving as if she answered to them, especially the head honcho, Richmond Vale.

But she wasn't willing to take orders from a bunch of elected civilians—and that chafed the delicate hides of the rich old men who thought they were still running a good ole boys club.

She scanned Hoyt up and down. Late forties, born and raised in town...worked under the former sheriff who might've been working with them.

"How about you go out there and have a talk with him." She said it like a statement, though, not a question, leaving little room to wiggle out of the task.

Hoyt sat back, rubbing his palms on his pants. "Talk with him or interrogate him?"

"I'll leave that up to you to decide." She grabbed the recorder from earlier and slid it over. It was slim enough that it could fit into his pocket without any problems. Resolving the issue of not having body cams was rocketing up her to-do list. "Make sure you get everything recorded, though. So nothing you say can be used against you later."

6

Hoyt understood why West had sent him on this call. But his disdain for Mitchell Longfellow was only marginally less than his boss's. Recalling how the Yacht Club had tried to destroy his marriage, Hoyt considered leaving without speaking to the man. While they lacked concrete evidence of his involvement with the elitist thugs, there was no doubt in Hoyt's mind that the man was corrupt. West would understand, he hoped.

Instead, he sighed and continued up the walkway.

The Select Board's treasurer's house wasn't on par with the McMansions in Sandcastle Court, but it was nicer than the houses in Sunrise Terrace. It was an older home that had been remodeled and upgraded over the years, and Hoyt could remember at least two times since he'd been on the force when he'd seen construction teams working on it.

The three-car garage could be hiding the brand-new Tesla he knew Longfellow drove and the Land Rover his wife owned. Hoyt's cruiser, with a slightly smashed grill guard, was entirely out of place parked in front of it.

He walked up to knock on the door. The doorbell was

one of those that recorded video and had an intercom as well. Just in case, he pressed the button there too.

Hoyt was a little surprised at how quickly the door swung open.

Longfellow stood inside, staring up at him. For someone who liked to think he was a "big man" in island politics, he was short in stature. Add in the rumpled shorts and t-shirt he wore, and Hoyt felt like he had the upper hand.

"Deputy Frost, there had better be a good reason you're ringing my doorbell on a weekend afternoon. I only work Monday through Friday, not on Saturdays."

Forcing his hands to relax at his sides, Hoyt strained to keep his cool.

He'd told West they weren't at odds, but that was before coming face-to-face with Mitch, knowing it was very likely this man was involved in the Yacht Club. The same Yacht Club he now believed nearly destroyed his marriage when they paid a woman to seduce him years ago. He'd never forget the look on Angie's face when she saw those damn pictures. He'd spent years trying to make up for his indiscretion, but he'd never get over how much a fool he felt for falling into their honeypot trap.

But he couldn't go and piss the man off right away, especially since he currently couldn't prove Mitch Longfellow had anything to do with any of that mess. There'd be time for that later.

"This isn't about city duties. I'm here on official police business, investigating a case."

Longfellow sighed with gusto and threw his hands up. "Fine. Whatever. Come on in." He turned and stomped into the house. "Do you want a beer?"

"No, thank you." Hoyt stepped in, glancing around the house. The floors were all hardwood and had an expensive gleam to them. Pieces of artwork decorated every wall, and there were several antiques in view. Wealth on display and plastered all over. "Like I said, I'm on official business."

"If you don't want a beer, fine, but you don't have to give me that lame excuse not to have one, Frost."

Hoyt ignored the strange statement.

Following Longfellow, he walked into a large living room where the board member had already stretched out in a leather recliner, sipping from a bottle of beer. Longfellow's TV had to be close to one hundred inches. A tiny stab of disgust pricked Frost as he saw it was being used to watch reruns of game shows in high definition.

"What can I do for Shadow Island's finest?"

"Did you hear about the man found on Beaman Beach this morning?"

Longfellow turned away from the screen. "What? No. Why is it since that woman took over for Alden, we've got dead bodies all over town? Can't you keep her in line?"

That sure is a familiar way to refer to the former sheriff of the island.

Hoyt fought back the urge to call him out on it. "I never said the person we found was dead, Mitch."

Hoyt did his best not to make the man's nickname sound like "bitch." For now. He hated when men talked so dismissively about women, and he learned—in that moment—he hated it even more when that woman was his boss. Still, he had to keep his words civil.

Mitch shrugged. "Well, it was implied. What happened?"

"Right now, it appears to be a boating accident of some kind." If he'd learned one very important thing from West, it was when to lie. This guy didn't deserve to know the truth.

"Oh, whatever, then. And, no, I haven't heard anything about it." Longfellow turned back to his program. "What does this man have to do with me?"

"Well, he's called you more than a few times over the last few days."

Longfellow waved him off. "I'm the treasurer of the Select Board. People call me all the time."

"Not the town hall or your office's number. It was this number. Your landline."

That finally got his attention, and Longfellow glared at Hoyt.

"My landline?" He shook his head. "I've been getting prank calls recently. Comes with the job, you know. People like to harass elected officials all the time. I hardly even use the landline. The only reason I have it is because it's required with my job."

Hoyt almost smiled as the man blustered through the excuse. He managed to keep his face neutral, though, as he turned his attention to the sports memorabilia littering the room.

As he let the silence work its magic, Hoyt couldn't help but wonder what being treasurer paid. Surely, Longfellow didn't make much more than he did. But there was no way he could afford to live in a house like this or buy even a few of the things he'd seen since walking through the front door. If his salary couldn't cover these expenditures, Hoyt guessed the bulk of Longfellow's income came in under the table.

Hoyt turned his focus back on Mitch, glad to see a light sheen of sweat on the man's forehead. "Maybe you know his name? The man was Chester Able."

"I don't know anyone named Able." Longfellow leaned back in his recliner. "And I've got no idea why he'd be calling me. You can write that in your case file and move on to your next lead. Sorry I can't be more help."

Hoyt moved to a bookcase, examining signed baseballs in glass cases and two vintage bats, but he could feel Longfellow's eyes on him. Good. Let him sweat a little more.

He squinted to make out the loopy script on one of the baseballs. It was signed by Ty Cobb. So was one of the bats. If these items were real, they had to be worth more than he himself made in a year. And board members didn't make more than sheriff deputies. The amount of money in this room made Hoyt's skin itch.

Hoyt faced Mitch again. "What did you talk to him about when he called?"

"I didn't. Why would I talk to some petty criminal?"

Hoyt's eyebrow arched. He'd never mentioned Chester Able was a criminal. "I didn't say—"

"None of this would be happening if Alden was still the sheriff. Or you were."

Hoyt ignored whatever subject Longfellow was hoping to broach. Hopefully, his antagonism for West was loud enough to be picked up by the recorder. "Chester wouldn't have been shot and left to die on a beach if Wallace was in charge? Is that what you mean?"

"Shot?" Longfellow twisted in his leather chair to stare at him. "What do you mean? I thought you said it was a boating accident."

Hoyt ignored that too. He'd been hoping to trip him up, but either he really didn't know what had happened, or Longfellow was a better actor than expected. A depressing third option was Hoyt wasn't very good at tricking folks. West always made it seem easy, since she lied so smoothly.

"Maybe it's the kind of accident that happens when someone is involved in the Yacht Club."

Mitch laughed and shook his head. A bead of sweat ran down his temple. "Of course I belong to a boat club. I'm docked at the Seaview Marina and enjoy the camaraderie of its membership. I've docked down there for years now. Not once, in all that time, have I heard of an accident like that. You need to stop listening to rumors and ghost stories. Do whatever you need to do to close the case and move on. Your sheriff needs to learn how to do her job properly as well."

He paused to take a sip of his beer then stared directly into Hoyt's eyes. "If she doesn't, well…the election for sheriff is only a few months away."

7

The tourists had taken over the beaches. This late in the season was always busy as people scrambled to get one last trip in before the summer was over. They made good cover as I got closer to the tiny crime scene that was blocked off on the north side of this stretch of sand.

But I couldn't get a good line of sight past the crime scene tape. If any of the bodies had washed to shore, I couldn't tell exactly where they'd landed.

A thirty-something woman lying on a brightly colored beach blanket while her children ran around in the surf peeked up from her book. She hadn't been reading it, not really. I saw her sneaking glances at the cops more often than she checked on her own kids. Nosy women were always the best way to get information.

"I wonder what's going on up there."

She jumped slightly when I spoke.

I knew what she saw. A basic man. I had basic looks and was wearing a baseball cap that completely covered my hair and the scar across my forehead. Plus, aviator glasses that hid half my face.

"I heard they found a body. It washed up from the ocean." Apparently, no one had told her not to speak to strangers.

"Really? Right there? Near those kids?" I pointed at the cluster of three kids, obviously hers, now digging up shells.

"No, where the tape is." She stared at her children playing in that same ocean and grimaced. "Maybe I should take my kids back to our rooms. Who knows what else could wash up? I don't want them mingling with dead bodies."

"Oh, I'm sure it's fine. The ocean's pretty big. No telling what could be in it. Plenty of bodies, I'd bet." I scratched my head as I took in the scene. There were a few people milling around closer to the tape, so I left the woman to see what else I could learn.

My phone beeped.

Do you have the information?

The number wasn't assigned, but I knew who the text was from.

Last night was supposed to be a straightforward task. Intercept the small yet growing group running cocaine from the Outer Banks to Baltimore, get the names of the suppliers, and report back to my contact in the Amado Cartel. They were displeased that their own business lines were being interrupted.

But instead of a small group of professionals, I found three guys who opted to piss their pants rather than answer a simple question.

However, there were more fish in the sea, as the saying went. Three terrified men did not make a drug-running empire. There were clearly others who would have that information. I just needed to get the rogue suppliers' names before the cartel decided I was incompetent.

They didn't tolerate incompetence.

I caught myself rubbing the scar on my forehead. It got itchy under the cap.

Soon, I texted.

Stepping into the loose crowd, I peeked over their heads. There was nothing on the sand. Not a single thing except people in full body suits digging and a single numbered marker. They had to be forensic techs. And they weren't finding anything. That was a good sign. Maybe this was related to what I'd done the night before, maybe it wasn't. What I'd told the woman was true. The ocean was a big place, and I wasn't the only one who used it to dump trash.

Two cops in uniform—and an older man in casual clothes who had to be a cop too—were standing around watching, both inside and outside the crime scene. I noticed one of the cops standing like a new military recruit. Legs spread, shoulders squared, hands crossed at the wrist held awkwardly in front of his belt buckle. Faint traces of bruises around his eye matched a split in his lip that was still healing.

Fragile ego. Too serious. Hot headed. Easy pickings.

I casually moved closer to him. "Oh my gosh, Officer, what happened? Is everyone okay?" I noted his name tag said Locke and nodded at where they were digging in the sand.

The deputy ignored me. Hell, he didn't even face me.

"Am I interrupting you, Deputy? I'm so sorry. I know you're busy…but it wasn't a shark attack or anything, right?" I put on my most concerned face.

The pompous fool turned his head to glare at me.

Apparently, he wasn't too sympathetic to public concern.

"Police business. Not yours."

I pretended to cower, holding my hands up and shaking them. "Ooh, police business. Didn't mean to intrude. We were all just curious. I heard there was a dead body found here and wanted to make sure my wife and kids were still safe. You know?" Twisting around, I pointed at the woman I'd been talking with.

"Police business. Move along." Deputy Pompous went back to staring straight ahead, ignoring me.

Another deputy walked over. His stride was smooth, his eyes saw everything, and he had his thumbs casually looped on his belt so both hands were close to his gun and Taser. This guy didn't appear to have a stick up his ass like this Locke guy.

"Can we help you?" His eyes were flat, but they roved over me, and I knew they were recording every detail. This cop—Deputy Hudson—was dangerous.

"No help needed, sir. I was just wondering what was going on here. Crime scenes can be rather scary to us civilians." I gave him my most pleasant "nothing to see here" smile, trying to throw him off track.

"Well, you can keep wondering from over there." Hudson jutted his chin out, pointing back to the fake wife I'd gestured toward earlier. This guy didn't miss a thing. "Unless you know something about what happened here today? What's your name, sir?"

I laughed that off. "I don't know anything. I was hoping you guys could tell me."

"What's your name, sir?"

His hands tightened slightly on his belt, and I knew I wasn't going to get anything useful from these guys.

"Name's Bob." I jerked my thumb over my shoulder. "My wife, Sheila, asked me to come see what's going on. She's worried about the kids, and maybe just a little bit nosy, if you know what I mean. She asked me to make sure there's nothing dangerous in the sand or water here."

"Nothing to worry about. Go on back to your wife and tell her that."

"Will do. And we'll keep the kids away, just in case. Thank you so much for your time. Sorry to have disturbed you, Deputies." I turned around and left them, but I could still feel their eyes on my back. No. Not theirs, just his. If I turned back, I was certain that first deputy would be too busy posing to pay attention to anything.

That Hudson guy was the real threat.

I hate cops.

I'd made it halfway to the road when I noticed someone running to catch up to me. For a second, I tensed, ready to fight to get away from the cops if I had to.

"Hey, man!" The voice didn't belong to either of the deputies, so I slowed and turned back.

A middle-aged man with a paunch and a fresh sunburn was coming in hot.

"Just wanted to let you know, the guy they found on the beach this morning made it."

That was not good news. "Sorry, what?"

"I overheard what you said about your family. I get that, man. My wife was worried, too, when we got here. But we heard a local found a man who'd had a boating accident. He was just lying on the beach early this morning. They think the tide pushed him in. He was taken to the medical center on the mainland, and the gossip going around is that he's gonna make it." He shrugged, acting as if he wasn't struggling to catch his breath after that short jog.

"A boating accident? Oh, that's terrible. But I guess that means those of us on shore are safe."

The tubby guy wheezed a laugh. "Yeah, we just need to stay away from boats."

I laughed, but inside, I was seething. Things were not going to plan if this was true and one of the guys I'd shot last night not only survived but made it to shore. No matter which idiot survived, it meant a headache, and he'd have to be taken care of.

But only one of them had the information I needed.

8

Rebecca stretched her back out, groaning as it refused to pop no matter how she twisted. Her office chair with lumbar support was a lifesaver, but it couldn't work miracles. She looked at the clock and saw it was past quitting time. The last few hours had been spent searching for Chester Able's next of kin. It'd been mostly fruitless.

His mother died years ago, and his father was unknown. He had one brother who was in jail, and a sister who'd been contacted but called back to tell Viviane she had no interest in getting involved in her brother's affairs.

As Chester was the victim of a crime and not a suspect, Rebecca couldn't force her to do anything. She'd broadened her search, hoping to find a spouse or even an ex who might know anything about medical history, who she could put in touch with his doctors, but there was no one.

Sighing, she picked up the phone to inform Coastal Ridge Hospital about her lack of results. The new doctor, Amanda Stuard, was busy, so she left the information with the staff instead. When she asked about his condition, they only said it was the same.

Hanging up, she started gathering her things. Until she had more information, or a different crime was uncovered, she might as well go home. At least there, she could check the files about the Yacht Club that Wallace had kept hidden—or maybe there was something in the logbooks they'd discovered under Jake Underwood's floor—and see if Chester was buried in one of those reports.

Footsteps echoed down the hall, and she paused, waiting to find out who had come in. Darian was scheduled to start his shift, but he was holding down the scene at the beach now that the forensic team had shown up. Hoyt paused in her doorway and shook his head as soon as he saw her watching.

"You couldn't get in contact with Mitchell Longfellow?"

Hoyt threw himself down in his chair and pulled the audio recorder from his pocket. "Oh, I did. He was more concerned about watching his damn game shows than anything else, though."

Rebecca could tell there was more to it and sat down as well. "Tell me about it."

"He said he had nothing to do with the criminal, Chester Able. Problem is, I never mentioned Able's criminal history." He slid the recorder across her desk. "I recorded the whole thing. There's a lot on there. Including him implying that if Wallace was still in your seat, he wouldn't have to answer any of my questions. He also implied that if I were in your seat, I wouldn't ask these questions either."

"Really?" She took the recorder and plugged it into her computer, readying it to copy the audio file over. "Did he explain why?" They both knew Wallace had hidden a lot of things, but neither of them could figure out what his intentions were.

Wallace had filed reports like he should have for years, but so many of those cases were tossed out of court on technicalities. He'd once confided to her that the reasons the cases had been tossed didn't make sense. And it'd happened at a higher incident rate than other cases moving through the justice system. After he and his staff had been threatened, he'd stopped filing the cases with the courts but still wrote everything down and kept the records hidden in a storeroom only he had access to.

It was those files that Rebecca was wading through to piece together the spiderweb of drug dealers, traffickers, and elite rich men who made up the Yacht Club, which preyed on the residents of Shadow Island and who knew where else.

"Not exactly. He dodged my questions about the Yacht Club, instead saying that he docked his boat down at the marina. Like he was using *Yacht Club* but with lower case emphasis, if you know what I mean. I got a bad feeling from that conversation. It was like Mitch was trying to get at something with me but not really saying it."

He rubbed his jaw, letting Rebecca know he had more. "I did have a good chance to inspect the front rooms of his house a bit. Either town treasurers get paid a lot more than you and I put together, which they do not, his wife won the lottery, or someone else is supplementing his income on a shocking scale."

Rebecca knew how to answer at least two of those questions and started searching the internet. "What reason did he give for Able calling him so often?"

Hoyt rolled his eyes. "Can you believe he tried to say that he'd been getting prank calls? That was the reason Able was calling. To prank an elected official of a tiny town nowhere near where he lived."

She chuckled and finished clicking through websites. "Prank calls that lasted several minutes each and only came through late in the evening?"

"Well, I didn't tell him we knew how long the calls were."

She found the page she wanted. "City treasurer income is public knowledge, and he makes only a hair less than I do currently." With that covered, she lifted her gaze to him. "You think that was basic misogyny or because he misses having someone in charge that will bend to their whims and take orders?"

"Oh, he's for sure a misogynist."

She was pleased but not surprised to see he was disgusted by that. Anyone who was married to Angie couldn't pretend that women were lesser unless they had their heads firmly planted up their own butts.

"In fact, he wanted to know why I couldn't keep you in line."

Rebecca snorted at the idea. Hoyt was an extremely competent cop and filled in when she was out for any reason, but he was the last person in the station who wanted the complex responsibilities of being sheriff. In fact, he'd rejected the job when Wallace died. Still, she couldn't help but tease him. "You want this seat?"

"I'd rather take early retirement." Hoyt's answer was immediate and emphatic. "At least now when I screw up, I can blame you for it."

"Sheriff, you got your ears on?" Darian's voice came from the radio she kept on her desk.

She picked up the mic. "I never seem to take them off anymore, Hudson. What's up?"

"Staties have made landfall, sir. Thought you'd want to know."

Rebecca frowned at the *sir*. Darian usually only did it when he was replying to her, or she was giving him orders. Or when something was going wrong and had him up on his toes. Could he be starting to lose it being around the sand for so long? He'd already been out there facing his triggers for several hours now.

"Is that all?" There was a long pause. "Talk to me, Hudson. What's happening?"

"We had a man approach the barrier earlier. Might be nothing. But I'd like to speak to you face-to-face about it."

There was a strange enough tone in his voice that Rebecca was at once standing up. "We're on our way. Hold tight."

P ulling onto the side of the road closest to the crime
   scene, Rebecca hopped out of her cruiser and headed
straight toward her men. Darian's unwillingness to talk over
the radio had set her nerves on edge. He'd never acted that
way before.

She crested the dune and took stock of the situation.
State police were milling around, most of them grouped
together off to the side. Boats were gathering as well, with
nets ready to start dragging the shallows.

Special Agent Rhonda Lettinger from the Norfolk State
Police Bureau of Criminal Investigation was there too.
Rhonda had proven to be a great resource, and Rebecca was
glad to see her on the scene. She was standing next to Darian
and Greg, chatting away with a radio in one hand and a
phone in the other as she coordinated everyone's
movements.

As Rebecca marched down the dune, they finally noticed
her.

"What's up?" She looked between her men and the state
police agent.

"I'll go get Locke. He's the one who noticed it, so he should be the one to tell you." Greg walked over to where Locke was still standing guard at the south side of the scene.

Rebecca raised an eyebrow and cocked her head at Darian.

At her look, he answered her original question. "I'm not sure yet. Hear what we have to say and tell us what you think. You've got more experience with things like this, I'm guessing."

That put her a bit more at ease. Still, she couldn't help but glance at his feet. Darian's boots were tied tight against his trousers. It was a good solution to his problem, and she ignored it from that point on. He would tell her if he was having issues.

"Evening, Sheriff." Rhonda still had both her hands full but was no longer focused on the devices. "I'm starting to wonder if maybe I should have a part-time rental down here, as often as we get called out."

"We do seem to be having more than our fair share of problems this summer." Rebecca tried to smile but knew it would be strained at best. She often struggled to hide her reactions.

"Oh, I'm just busting your chops." Rhonda smirked.

"Maybe you are, but I've heard that same sentiment from your men plenty already."

"My men?" Rhonda turned, hands on hips, and glared at the men. "Those aren't my men. Anyone who worked in the BCI branch of the VSP would know better than to stand around with their thumbs up their butts when there's actual work they should be doing." With every word, her voice got louder until it was clear the group could hear her.

Trading glances at each other, the staties finally broke up and moved off.

Rhonda smiled at Darian then turned to Rebecca. "I'll

have a word with the first sergeant. He and I are on good terms. And I know he's got a lot on his plate. That's one of the reasons he's fine with me popping down here. That, and we share the same currents, so we tend to have the same problems."

That was something Rebecca hadn't thought of before, but it made sense. The first time they'd worked together had been a case that originated in Norfolk and ended up on Shadow Island's shore. "And my jurisdiction ends just off the coast."

Rhonda sighed. "Yes, while ours goes to six miles off the coast, so it includes all the bays and waterways here. It's a big job, but we're up to the challenge." She glared at the few state troopers that were still in view. "At least, my team is. I don't know what's up with these guys here."

"They're right about one thing. We've called on them more than a few times the last couple of months." Most of the Shadow Island Sheriff's Department staff was already standing here, and they were completely outnumbered. Part of her wanted to explain the whole convoluted problem they were having that seemed to swirl around the Yacht Club.

Locke walked up while they were talking, moving slowly and keeping his head down as he stopped just outside their group.

Darian took matters into his own hands. "Locke, tell West about that guy from earlier."

Rebecca stared at him and waited.

He gulped, which was intriguing on its own. Locke always put on a tough-guy front. Now it was like he was reluctant to speak.

"It was a bit weird. I saw him walking up the beach, then he stopped to talk to a woman there alone with her kids. He lifted his hat to scratch his head and I noticed a scar on his forehead. A big one. After that, he walked right up, asking what was going on. I thought he was a busybody at first. He was nosy and, like, phony."

Her face went flat with annoyance, but she tried to stay focused. There was no way Darian and Greg would have suggested listening to him if he was only going to complain about people being rude.

"That's par for the course, but most people don't keep making up excuses. Still, just a weird guy, right? Except when he walked back to the woman he claimed was his wife, he never even talked to her. He left instead. When I realized he was gone, I got Hudson to stand in for me and I went to talk to her. Her name wasn't Sheila, like he'd said. She didn't even know the guy."

He side-eyed Darian, as if he needed encouragement.

Darian nodded. "Go on."

"She said basically the same thing happened with her. This guy walked up out of nowhere to ask about what was going on, then left."

Darian nodded. "Sir, I also didn't like the look of this guy. Something about him was off. I asked him his name, he said it was Bob, but he was lying about his own name too. I could tell. And he was watching me...gauging my reactions, how I moved. He was sizing me up."

Now, that was concerning. And Rebecca trusted Darian's assessment of people.

"Criminals often return to the scenes of their crimes, and he seemed quite interested in the goings-on." Locke pointed to himself and Darian. "We didn't tell him anything, Sheriff. Not a thing. Just told him to move along."

"Can either of you describe him?"

Locke squirmed. "His face was mostly covered, but like I said, he had a big scar on his forehead. And he was a bit taller than me."

Darian stepped forward. "I can work up a sketch on the program at the station."

Rebecca acknowledged what he'd said and took a moment to think about what to do next. "Go ahead and do that. Locke, go tell the troopers what he looks like so they can keep an eye out for him. Call me if you spot him again. Hudson, send out the image to everyone as soon as you have it."

"Yes, sir." Darian gave Locke an approving nod, a first as far as she knew, and headed for the cruisers, while the younger deputy took off at a jog toward the troopers.

"A random guy who puts one of your guys on edge snooping around our crime scene?" Rhonda shook her head. "I don't like the sound of that."

"Did you see that our victim has a rap sheet full of drug charges?" Rebecca turned away from the tourists, just in case. No one was paying undue attention to them, but it wasn't worth risking.

"I saw. I've already reached out to different stations on land, telling them to let me know if they get a floater. The currents are strong and swirl around the island."

"You think the other 'two' Chester talked about are dead already?"

Rhonda didn't answer right away. "You had your men check the rest of your beaches?"

Rebecca nodded. "And our fishing boaters checked the water. The Coast Guard's also been alerted. No one has spotted anything so far."

"Considering it's been around twelve hours since you found the first one, and we and the Coast Guard have had boats in the water, I'm not too hopeful we'll find them alive. Miracles do happen, though." Rhonda turned to face the water. "I'll have my guys check the smaller islands too. I suppose it could be possible they washed up there and that's why we haven't found anyone else yet. And I can ask the coasties to broaden their search into deeper water."

"Anything we can help with?" Rebecca's phone pinged, and she pulled it out of her pocket. Seeing a message from Ryker, she hoped Rhonda would say no.

"Nothing yet. I'm going to reach out to the Narc Squad too. Maybe they know of a reason why we've got a small-time drug dealer in the hospital."

10

"How's my favorite guy?" Rebecca got out of her truck in Ryker Sawyer's driveway.

At the sound of her voice, Ryker turned from where he was fiddling around in a flower bed, pulling a few weeds out. "Well, hey there." He smiled as a chocolate blur ran past him and jumped into Rebecca's arms as she knelt. "You were talking to Humphrey, weren't you?"

Rebecca laughed, turning her face up so she could talk while the chocolate lab bathed her face in puppy kisses. "He's so cute! How could I not be?"

Ryker abandoned his weedy garden and sauntered over to them, laughing as Humphrey's antics knocked Rebecca onto her butt. That worked out fine for both of them, as the lab attempted to fit his growing body onto her lap and settled for nibbling on her thumb instead. "He's been in a mood the last couple of days."

"I can see that." Rebecca pulled her hand out of the puppy's mouth, and he turned his attention to her shoes, gnawing on the edge of the sole. He sneezed, shaking his head, and she laughed again. "What's on the trailer?" She pointed at the new trailer parked next to his truck in the grass. It had something big and bulky hiding under a blue tarp.

"You know I don't always get paid for my work with cash?"

Rebecca nodded, unsuccessfully attempting to stand up with an energetic puppy fixated on her shoe now. Ryker was on retainer for general maintenance around town and, sometimes, did trades instead of taking payments from people who couldn't afford the work otherwise. However, she'd never seen him show up with anything that big.

"Well, I did some work at the dock, but they were tapped out on their insurance, so they gave me a boat instead." He helped her get back on her feet.

"Really?" She tried to picture what kind of boat could be under that tarp, but the shape was too distorted. The basic shape was there. The lumps could be the inflated tubes used as bumpers. The spines could be antennae or fishing poles, and the big one in back might be an outboard engine. "Is it seaworthy?"

"That depends on how you want to define *seaworthy*, I suppose." He laughed at the grim face she was making but got distracted when his phone started chiming. "It's good enough for two people to tool around the island in, so long as the waves don't get too high. And my timer is telling me dinner is ready."

Ryker started to walk inside, but Rebecca held out a hand and stopped him. When he looked back to see what was up, she stretched and kissed him. "How's my favorite *human* guy doing?" She winked as her gaze momentarily fell on Humphrey.

"Much better now." His lips brushed hers as he answered, and she felt them stretch into a smile. She kissed him again, and they didn't stop until Humphrey jumped up with his paws nearly reaching Ryker's chest, desperate to get between them.

"I probably shouldn't have said the d-word." At Rebecca's confused expression he explained with a smile. "Dinner."

Humphrey barked and ran for the door.

"I see what you mean." Hand in hand, they walked up the porch. As soon as Ryker opened the door, Humphrey bolted inside. The aroma of spicy cream sauce tantalized Rebecca's senses. "Oh, that smells delicious. What did you make?"

"Creamy Tuscan shrimp. I dropped the pasta in the water when you said you were coming over." Ryker let go of her hand to get Humphrey his food.

"I love shrimp. What's the special occasion?" Rebecca walked over and lifted the lid to enjoy the heavenly smells. The shrimp was already cooked and resting on a plate to the side of the stove. A big bowl of washed spinach sat next to it.

"You coming over for dinner." He gave Humphrey a pat on the rump and moved to join her. She stepped aside so he could finish cooking. "Honestly, though, this isn't anything special. I cook like this most nights."

Rebecca's eyes widened, and her mouth started watering at the thought of eating these types of meals every night. He noticed her and started laughing.

"I see the way to your heart really is through your stomach, isn't it?"

He was teasing her, but she decided to answer him seriously.

"It's not the food, per se. Though I will admit it does smell delicious. It's the idea of a home-cooked meal every night. Eaten on real plates. With the dog at our feet." She glanced wistfully over at Humphrey, who was inhaling his kibble.

Ryker set down the spoon he was using to fold the spinach and shrimp into the sauce, then he turned and held her hands. "What you're talking about is 'home.' Family meals, sharing your day, someone to come home to."

Realizing he was right, Rebecca's cheeks grew hot. This was what she'd actually been searching for when she left D.C. and came down here. When she'd chosen where to go, she'd thought she'd only be able to find good memories. Instead, she'd reconnected with Ryker and started something she'd never expected.

"So, uh, did I tell you about my most recent case?" It was a cowardly thing to do, but she wasn't ready to talk about her feelings or what was growing between them. For the last two weeks, they'd spent more nights together than alone. It'd happened so easily that she hadn't even noticed until he brought it to her attention. Now her feelings were so big they'd become the elephant in the room. At least, in her head.

His eyes sparkled with humor, and she knew he understood why she was changing the subject. "No. Why don't you tell me about it while you drain the pasta?"

Rebecca opened a cupboard door and pulled out the colander. "Kelly Hunt, I think you know her, she's my neighbor, was walking her dog, Brody, like they do every morning, when she found a man washed up on the beach. It seems he might have a connection with Mitchell Longfellow. And then Longfellow said the most disturbing thing about Wallace too."

"Oh, do tell." When she handed him the bowl of drained pasta, he poured the sauce over the top and started folding it all together. "Can you get the plates down?"

As she set the table and got out his favorite beer and one of her coffee stouts he kept in the fridge now, she told him about finding Mitchell Longfellow's number in the call log and how Hoyt's interview with him went and what the man had implied.

Ryker listened, seemingly intrigued by this strange turn

of events. By the time she'd finished the story, they were seated at the table and half done with their meal. Humphrey was curled up in his usual spot under the table where he could touch both their feet.

"You know, I know Mitch. Professionally, at least."

Rebecca raised her eyebrows, her mouth full of pasta. "Really?"

"Yeah, he's the one who gets my invoices and makes sure I get paid by the city. He didn't seem that bad to me, but he's clearly a toady of Richmond Vale's. I had no idea he was quite so shady, though. Never even heard a rumor about that."

"Well, don't let that get out."

Ryker shook his head and leaned back, taking a sip of his beer. "Of course I won't. But what's this about Wallace? He never worked with them. I know you didn't get to know him well before he passed, but the Wallace I knew couldn't stand guys like Vale and Longfellow. He always said they were bureaucratic pains in his ass."

She sighed and pushed the rest of her pasta around her plate, picking out the shrimp to devour first. "We don't know. There's nothing to say Wallace was on the take, but there's also not a lot of evidence showing he was clean either."

"Did you consider he might *not* have been on the take, exactly? There's one club here older than the Yacht Club, you know."

"I didn't know." She dropped a shrimp back onto her plate, interested to hear about this other possibility.

"The good ole boys club. Nothing has a longer history or a more toxic atmosphere than that. A man Wallace's age, there's no possibility he wasn't involved in that. He might've been doing favors and never really saw them as all that bad. Certainly not corrupt."

Rebecca chewed that over. The "good ole boy" mindset was something she'd run into fairly often in her career. Hell, most men didn't see anything wrong with it or how harmful the social phenomenon was.

After all, they were doing a favor for the son of their friend or grandson or whomever. She'd seen plenty of cops sully their reputations "looking out for" other police officers who'd done the wrong thing, even though they would've thrown the book at a private citizen who acted in the same fashion.

Some of Wallace's actions had been done to save his best friend, Hoyt Frost, when he got caught in a honeypot trap. And Trent Locke had been hired on the force because of someone pulling strings as well. Darian Hudson had been hired solely for his own accomplishments and his standing as a "returning son" after separating from the Army. But after being forced to hire Locke, Wallace hadn't hired another person, even though he had the budget and the need for another deputy.

"I know that face. You've thought of something new, haven't you?" Ryker stood and started collecting the dishes.

Rebecca bobbed her head absentmindedly. When she'd started going through the folders Wallace had left her, she'd assumed, as Hoyt had, that they were out of order because they weren't chronological. But what if, instead, they had been filed that way on purpose? In a way that made sense to someone who knew about the good ole boy's club.

11

R ebecca still had another forty-five minutes before she needed to be at work. She'd swung by her house to get a change of clean clothes, but since she was already running ahead of schedule and hadn't gotten any updates on the search, she decided to also swing by the crime scene.

Even from the road, she could tell the search was ongoing. The tall masts of the U.S. Coast Guard bobbed above the dunes. She parked on the side of the road after spotting Rhonda camped out in her car. Grabbing a cup carrier with a pastry bag nestled between three steaming cups, she climbed out of her cruiser and went to join her.

"Morning, Sheriff." Rhonda had her windows down, basking in the cool morning breeze while working on her laptop.

"Morning, Agent." She grinned, enjoying being called Sheriff a lot more than she ever liked being called Agent. While the BCI special agents had smaller jurisdictions, they did much the same work she used to do on a federal level.

"We've worked together long enough, you think we can do away with titles and surnames?" Rhonda faced her. "I get called Lettinger so often I'm starting to forget it's not my first name."

Rebecca laughed. "You're not the only one. I think only my boyfriend and my neighbor call me Rebecca anymore."

"Boyfriend? That's a new development, isn't it?" She grinned as Rebecca's cheeks turned pink.

Although she already felt a strong kinship with Rhonda, she grimaced at having blurted out the moniker for Ryker. It was crazy how strong her feelings were for the man in her life, and it definitely scared her. "First time I've called him that too."

"That does explain why you were driving to your house so early this morning." Rhonda teased, looking back at her screen as dots moved about on the map. It had to be the ships out doing the searches.

"Or I could've been getting you a muffin and a cup of coffee before coming over here." The lie slipped easily off Rebecca's tongue.

"Could've been, except I had to pass your house on the way here at dawn and your truck wasn't in your driveway." Still, Rhonda leaned her head out the window. "Did you really get me a muffin?"

"Or a doughnut. Whichever you prefer." Rebecca was more than willing to let the topic change. "I hit up the Bean Tree Coffeehouse. They make the best pastries in the state, and their coffee is top notch too."

"How could I say no to something like that?" Rhonda set aside her laptop and twisted in her seat. "Your man Hudson's here too. Is that who the third cup's for?"

Rebecca stepped back to let her open the door and set their breakfast down on the hood of her SUV. "Yup, I'll call him over."

While Rhonda doctored her coffee and chose her pastry, Rebecca called Darian to come join them. He was over the dune and reaching for the cup before Rhonda had taken more than a single bite.

"Anything new?" Darian reached into the bag and made his selection without looking, chugging the coffee black.

"Nothing from my end. I was going to wait 'til nine to call and check on Chester since I didn't get an update through the night. I know he was going in for surgery yesterday, so at this point no news is good news."

"We've covered 'most everything we can with the drag nets. The scuba divers are already suited up to search the deeper areas. They've been at it since sunrise." Rhonda wiped her lips with a paper napkin. "I'm overseeing them from here since this is the only confirmed location. A wounded man couldn't swim very far, so we checked the currents that might've helped him reach this spot."

Darian grunted into his cup, sending up a spout of steam from the lid. "Except there're so many around the island, and the island is small enough, he could've come from anywhere around us."

Rhonda nodded. "And that's the problem. Here's the area where your man might've gone into the water." She reached into her cruiser and pulled out her laptop, showing the map on the screen.

"That's the entire bay and coast of the mainland." Rebecca recalled the unwelcome gift the hurricane had dumped on their shores a month ago. Two bloated, fish-eaten corpses dredged up from the bottom of the ocean and separated from their boat that wound up on Little Quell Island. Currents made tracking maritime crimes impossible.

Wrinkling her nose, Rhonda pointed. "And the bridges. I've already sent the troopers to search up and down those to look for signs of a struggle. They came up with nothing. But you see why this is taking so long. We've also checked the logs for trips in the area, but nothing stood out."

"What about the drug-running aspect of this?" Rebecca noted that a third of the search area was green with the rest of the area in red, showing the search progress.

"I'm coordinating with the DEA on that. We work together fairly often already, but I wanted to double-check with them. They said the trafficking has slowed down a bit since you took down that group of human traffickers and the FBI started poking its nose into things. By the way, I didn't thank you for that. I got to clean up the rest of the group after you took down the head man."

Bringing down the men who'd been profiting from the sale of children had been a personal highlight in Rebecca's career. She could still hear the frightened whimpers of the three girls she'd saved that night. Anything to make sure that didn't happen to more children from her island.

"Glad to be of service. These things do tend to snowball. They also tend to leave vacuums in the supply chain."

"Which means we might be dealing with someone new." Rhonda popped the last bite of pastry into her mouth.

"And that means we don't know where they travel, what they're moving, how they go about things, or who they are." Darian shrugged and reached for the bag again. "Snafu."

Rhonda frowned at him over her cup, and Rebecca translated.

"Situation normal, all fucked up."

12

Hoyt sat at his desk. He should've been working, but he couldn't get his mind to focus. All night long, he'd had terrible dreams, which clung to him...

He and Alden Wallace, his boss and best friend, sat on a porch drinking beers and talking. Darian joined them. Just some good ole boys enjoying beers after work. People appeared in the yard. A man with a gun walked up. But Hoyt wasn't afraid.

The man talked to Alden, but his voice was muffled.

Then the man turned. He took a young woman, who was magically standing in the yard, and they disappeared.

A middle-aged couple appeared and started crying as if their hearts were broken.

Alden kept talking like nothing was happening.

The vague knowledge of a threat—unseen, unknown—approached. Alden somehow deflected that danger to one of the now numerous people in his yard.

In the back of his mind, Hoyt knew his wife was safely inside. His sons were out of town. They were all safe.

He watched, over his beer bottle, from his comfortable chair, as one random person in his yard after the next vanished to never return. Sometimes, he recognized the person. Cassie. Nevaeh. Dan. That printshop kid who'd helped put up flyers. The boy whose puppy was stolen. Family members of those taken started popping up in clumps in place of those who'd vanished, and they were crying. Their numbers grew until his yard was filled with mourners.

Then he'd woken up, but he couldn't shake the feeling.

Alden had died barely one month ago. And Hoyt was still grieving. Not even just because he was dead, but because his best friend might not have been the man Hoyt thought he was.

He was killed by the same men he protected—willingly or not— all those years.

Sitting at his desk, he stared at the open case file on his computer screen. He should've been writing a report about Longfellow's taped interview—making it official, what the man had said about the late sheriff.

Instead, his mind refused to stray from Alden and the gaps in police files. Hoyt knew for a fact, just over a year ago, they'd had a man wash up on the shore. He'd been first on scene. He'd even started the case file. But Alden had showed up and taken over.

Hoyt never saw or heard about that man again.

A tiny shiver of dread shook his spine as he gave up on writing the report and, instead, did a search. He remembered the exact date.

Nothing.

No report. No follow-up. No record of even calling for medical attention. Which meant that man was yet another case kept hidden by Alden, tucked away somewhere in the paper files. He wouldn't even know if the man survived unless he managed to find the report. Which meant Alden was willing to hide even major cases.

Worse, Alden had lied to him, telling him the Feds had taken over the case. Or some shit like that.

And I'd believed him.

Guilt sat heavy on Hoyt's shoulders, bowing them down and making it hard to breathe. Rebecca's words, from when she'd faced down the Yacht Club thugs on her own, had stuck with him.

"No, Deputy Frost, you're the one not taking this seriously enough. You and this entire department have not taken this seriously enough for the last thirty years. At least. You've allowed criminals to invade your town. They're a threat to everyone on this island and the surrounding areas, while you've only cared about yourself and your coworkers. Wallace protected you guys, but who was protecting Cassie when she needed it? Or Serenity? And who knows how many others!"

He knew her admonition was the cause of his nightmares. The worst part was that he deserved the restless sleep. Every sleepless night was one he'd earned with years of complacency.

There's no rest for the wicked. Even those who sin by turning a blind eye.

Hoyt stared at the wall opposite the dispatch desk. From his seat, he couldn't see it, but he knew what was there. Every morning when he came in, except for today, he'd looked at the face of Sheriff Alden Wallace, lost in the line of duty. A tribute to a fallen hero.

Rebecca had commissioned that plaque.

"Out of everyone living, you probably knew my brother the best." The words from Alden's brother, Tom, came back to him.

Shoving his seat back, Hoyt stormed out of the bullpen, pushed his way through the half door, and stared at that plaque.

Serving with Integrity, Honor, and Commitment.

"Hoyt, are you okay?" There was a heavy thread of worry in Viviane's voice, but he ignored her.

"Honor. How honorable were you, to have allowed so many crimes to go unpunished?" The guilt eating at him turned into rage. He wanted to punch Alden in the face, or at least in his unjustified memorial. Demand answers for what he'd been hiding. "You don't deserve this damn plaque, Alden. Maybe it's time we take it down."

The door behind him swung open.

"Frost, are you okay?"

The sheriff's voice got through to him, and he turned on her. Her light brown eyes showed worry, and an eyebrow lifted at his aggressive motions.

Viviane sat at her desk, staring at them with wide, worried eyes and twisting her fingers around each other.

"No. I'm not okay." Hoyt yanked his badge from his chest. It felt like he was tearing his own heart out. He held it up. "I knew Alden better than anyone. I knew what made him tick. I knew what he would and wouldn't do. But every case since his death, I find myself doubting him all over again."

"Har—"

"This is supposed to mean something." His fingers clenched around his badge, and he glared at it. He knew he could break it, bend it, destroy it. It was so flimsy. "The one you wear, the one he wore, should mean even more. The man I thought I knew would not have done the things..." He couldn't say it. "He wouldn't have. But—"

"But nothing." Rebecca grabbed the fist clutching his badge. She pulled him around and somehow, despite her smaller hands, managed to twist it out of his hold. She shoved a paper bag from Bean Tree Coffeehouse into his grasp, then spun him so he was facing the half door. "Take this and go sit at your desk. I'll be right in."

"What?" Try as he might, Hoyt couldn't keep up with what was going on.

"Go." Rebecca shoved him, making him step forward, and pulled her phone from her pocket.

Defeated, Hoyt followed orders. He didn't look up as Viviane buzzed him through.

Following the well-worn track of countless days of habit, he sat at his desk. The warmth from the bag and the tantalizing smells coming from within didn't do anything to ease his funk.

He simply sat limply in his chair. His eyes refused to focus on anything. The urge to scream and cry, rage against reality, and deny his friend's culpability—his own—waged war inside his mind, drowning everything else out.

"Frost?"

Hoyt lifted his eyes.

Darian stood next to his desk, dressed in a tank top and cargo shorts, apparently ready to cut out. He nodded to the bag.

"Huh?"

"You plan on sharing those or are you going to hog them all?"

"What?"

Darian pulled his chair over. "Boss said we're having a staff meeting. I'm assuming she bought breakfast for all of us since she called this last minute." He took a bear claw.

Shell-shocked, Hoyt looked around. Viviane and Rebecca were walking over.

"I've locked up. It's a Sunday morning. If anyone needs us, they can use the button outside. Everyone, have a seat."

Rebecca stood over Hoyt. "You're going to need to hold onto this." She slapped his badge into his palm.

Rebecca sat on the spare desk at the front of the bullpen, resting her feet on the chair.

Viviane grabbed Greg's chair and moved it next to Darian, sitting in it before she took the bag from him.

"What I'm about to tell you goes no further than this room."

"Shouldn't we wait for Abner and Locke?" Darian looked toward the door.

Hoyt's stomach twisted. Darian said this was a staff meeting. If so, why was she leaving one-third of them out of it?

"No. Once I explain, you'll see why. Frost, I need you to listen to what I'm about to say and not lose your cool. If you can't do that, I'll accept your badge back whenever you want to rid yourself of it."

Darian and Viviane jerked and turned to stare at him. Hoyt's blood slowed, his heart seizing.

"All right."

"Hudson, Darby, the same goes for you two." That had to be the first time she'd referred to Viviane by her last name.

Darian squared his shoulders. "Yessir."

"Yes, ma'am." Viviane nodded sharply, bracing herself, even though she didn't have a badge to worry about.

"Let me be blunt so there's no misunderstanding." Rebecca folded her hands together. "Sheriff Alden Wallace was corrupt. He worked with the Yacht Club to keep their people out of jail."

Hoyt felt like the bottom had just fallen out of his world. Viviane and Darian didn't look much better.

"Please, God, no," Viviane whispered.

"As terrible as his decisions were, I think he might've done them for what he thought was a good reason." She rubbed her hands together. "Frost showed me where Wallace hid his reports, the ones that involved the Yacht Club and were never properly filed with the courts. It took me a long time to figure it out, but I think I did." She took a deep breath. "And that's where things get tricky. But where the three of you might be able to shed some light."

"Sir?" Darian's eyes were dark and hard enough to chip granite.

"None of the victims in the reports he hid were locals." Her eyes seemed to bore a hole right through Hoyt.

Hoyt remembered what Tom had said at the memorial, and it all made a terrible kind of sense. "Alden didn't have any kids. Once he became sheriff, he saw the island as his family, and he was adamant about protecting everyone on it."

Rebecca nodded. "That's what I thought too. Do you think he could've done what he did to protect you guys, the locals, the people he considered family?"

"Yes, sir."

"Oh, yeah."

Hoyt nodded slowly. That, sadly, all made sense. "That sounds like the man I knew."

Rebecca looked at each one of her coworkers. "And that's where his corruption ended."

"What do you mean?" Hoyt could barely get the words out.

"Frost, you remember when you handed me Wallace's secret files? You said they were out of order, and it was probably because he ran out of space and started jamming them in wherever they would fit?"

He nodded as the others stared at him. This was the first time they'd heard of it. "Yeah."

"We had it wrong. Wallace wasn't filing in chronological order. He was trying to find everyone involved. So he filed them according to who they were connected to. Wallace was putting together a case, not to take down one or two people at a time. Those cases got tossed out of court when he tried. He planned to take them *all* down at once."

Hoyt didn't understand. "He would've told me."

Rebecca drank from her cup of coffee then let out a long, deep sigh. "It appears he was putting together a Federal RICO case that would've taken him down as well."

Darian slapped his hands together in a thunderous clap. He turned to Hoyt with a huge smile. "I knew it! That bastard was playing them."

Fuck.

Hoyt's ears started ringing as it all came together in his mind. "And if he had told us, we would've been just as guilty as he was."

Viviane gasped.

Rebecca just looked at him.

Darian stopped celebrating. His face fell. "Guilty? What?"

"Alden filled out all the reports. He took over the scenes. He gathered the evidence. He did that to protect us while he was covering for their crimes." Hoyt watched as Rebecca met their gazes, one by one. "I'm betting he had a deal with the Yacht Club that they'd leave the locals alone. When he thought they broke that deal with Cassie's murder, he went after them. And he did it in a way so that none of his people would be exposed to the danger or corruption."

"Boss?" Viviane raised a hand, which shook as much as her voice. "Why aren't Locke and Abner here?"

Hoyt jerked upright. Locke. He was the one who'd been with Alden when he died. He'd been in on the planning for the meeting that went bad. Locke had left his friend lying in the sand where he'd been shot.

"I didn't call Abner because he's retired. There's no reason to bring him into this mess right now."

"And Locke?" Darian's voice was so cold, it should have turned the bullpen into an ice rink.

She shrugged. "I have no evidence against him. And he proved on the last case that he had my back. But his training appears to have been either corrupt or incomplete. I need to rectify that but haven't had the time."

"Do you think Locke's a...?" Viviane bit her lip.

"I don't know. He could just be incompetent."

Darian snorted. "He's definitely incompetent...but you said he followed your directions when he was your backup in the marsh."

Hoyt couldn't think of a thing to say. He didn't want to work with a corrupt deputy, having to trust him when lives were on the line. But if Rebecca had trusted him...that said a lot.

"Until I'm certain he's not working with the Yacht Club, I'm not ready to trust him with this information."

"But you trust us." Viviane was beaming at Rebecca.

"With my life." The smile she gave in response was full of pride.

It made Hoyt remember when he'd been the rookie and Sheriff Wallace had said he trusted him for the first time. That had been the start of their friendship that lasted until death.

"What..." He coughed to clear his throat. "What do we do now?"

Rebecca turned to him. "Now we keep sorting, putting together all the information Wallace compiled for us. And," she glanced up at the clock, "I keep rattling their chains. They think they have power over us, but they're wrong. And I think it's about time I remind them of that."

———

13

Richmond Vale scowled as he opened the door and saw Rebecca standing there. His back straightened. His attempt to look dignified in his unwrinkled t-shirt and Bermuda shorts was enough to make her smile. His house was only a few doors down from Longfellow's and on the other side of the street. It also had a ridiculously large-lion head door knocker that she'd been thrilled to slam against his door repeatedly.

"I don't work from home, Sheriff, or on the weekends. If you need me for something, make an appointment with my secretary." He sniffed at her.

He started to swing the door shut, but she slapped a hand against it, holding it open. "That sounds lovely, but I don't get weekends off. And this is an official visit."

Vale sneered at her hand pressed against his door and even tried to push it shut again.

Rebecca didn't budge.

He sighed and rolled his eyes so dramatically it would've put a teenager to shame.

"Mitchell Longfellow is a person of interest in an

attempted murder case."

The pushing stopped as Vale's mouth fell open. "That can't—"

"Were you with him the night before last at nine?" The time was completely irrelevant. She had nothing to lead her to believe Longfellow was the shooter either. All she wanted to know was how far Vale would be willing to go to cover for the man.

Vale shuffled around, calculating his answer. "At nine? I think so. Not in person. We were on the phone."

It was a good lie. Enough to cover for Longfellow, while also covering for himself. Too bad it was also one she could easily check. "On his cell phone or home phone number?"

"I...I'm not sure." He waffled his hand in the air. "Whatever number I have for him in my cell phone."

Rebecca nodded and pulled out her notepad. "So you called him from your cell phone and were on the phone with him at nine?" She clicked her pen and held it over the page, smiling at him while he glared from his front door.

He paused, looking at her pen as if it were a bug. "Why are you taking notes?"

She flipped the pen around. "Would you prefer I record this instead?"

Vale smirked at her and her pen. "How would you do that? You haven't even bought those body cameras yet."

Her hand stilled. She'd gotten the budget for the cameras cleared weeks ago but had something much better in mind. Her plan was to buy something without Vale knowing. Keep it off the books and off his radar. Then maybe, just maybe, the man would slip up and she'd capture it. But her alternate plan was taking longer than she wanted. She made a mental note to see if she could expedite the arrangements. "And how do you know that?"

He raised his arm and leaned on the edge of the door. "I'm

Chairman of the Select Board. I know everything that happens in my town."

"Then you also know why Longfellow said that if Wallace was still in charge, he wouldn't have to answer any questions about this investigation?" She phrased it as a question and returned his smirk when he jolted back, making the door swing in its frame.

"Because he's an idiot. But being an idiot isn't a reason to investigate him for attempted murder."

Rebecca ignored that. "Which means you do know why he said that. What reason could he have to believe that the previous sheriff wouldn't follow leads in this case?"

"Because he would be smart enough to look for *viable* leads instead of harassing influential men in the community that you should know better than to annoy."

"Influential?" Rebecca raised her eyebrow in her best Dwayne "The Rock" Johnson impersonation. "He's treasurer of a town so small it's not even a city. We don't even have a full handful of stoplights."

Vale was getting more spun up the more she talked, and that only added to the smug feeling she no longer tried to hide from him.

"The number of stoplights we have isn't relevant to his presence on the Select Board. And you would be wise to remember his status. As your continued presence on our little island can be erased if either one of us decides to back a different candidate."

"If you want my job, run against me in November." She waved away his threat.

"I don't think you understand the power the Select Board holds."

Rebecca shook her head and used the voice she knew would annoy him the most. "And I'm surprised you don't know the limits of your power. To get me out of office, you need a majority." She paused, waiting for him to open his mouth so she could cut him off. "Of the registered county voters. Not the Select Board."

She let that sink in.

However, Vale wasn't as cocksure as she had thought and was visibly struggling. "We'll see," was all he offered.

"Is that why Longfellow thought Wallace wouldn't investigate him? Because he thought he had the power to illegally remove an elected official from office on a whim? I hope Wallace didn't think the same thing. The bylaws regarding the employment of the county sheriff are more than twenty years old at this point. Longfellow has only been serving for nine years. He never had that kind of power over Wallace."

Vale's face turned blotchy as he flushed with anger and paled with fear simultaneously. "Listen—"

"The name of the person who nominates candidates is also public record. And don't worry, I've already made copies of it in case it goes missing."

His eyes narrowed and he opened his mouth to respond but seemed to struggle for the words.

Before he could, her radio crackled to life. "Sheriff, the divers have an update on the case. They're waiting for you."

She'd warned everyone she was going to be at Vale's house and not to interrupt unless it was an emergency. Even then, they weren't to give any information that could clue him into what was happening. Just by saying it was the divers let Rebecca know they'd recovered bodies.

Picking up her radio, she held it to her mouth while keeping her eyes locked on Vale. "On my way, dispatch." She released the toggle and gave Vale the tiniest of nods. "We'll finish this conversation later."

She turned and strode to her Explorer. Several seconds went by, long enough for her to make it halfway to her sheriff's cruiser that she'd parked on the road for everyone to see.

The crack of his door slamming shut made her sigh with satisfaction.

Now that she'd shoved it in his face just how little power he had, Vale would be running scared. And scared criminals were more likely to make mistakes.

Or retaliate.

Climbing into her vehicle, a thought flitted up from the back of her mind. Something her instructors had warned her about at Quantico.

A man who could lose everything if he's caught has nothing to lose when fighting to get away.

14

Rebecca nodded to Hoyt, who was the first person to notice her as she walked to where they were beaching the search boats. It wasn't far from where they'd found the original body. They were on the same beach, but farther south, where the M.E. would be able to meet them to pick up the bodies without a long hike through the sand.

"How'd it go, Boss?"

Rhonda looked over as well, away from the boat that was being pulled onto the sand.

"About as well as could be expected." Rebecca had to shade her eyes with her hand as she walked toward the midmorning sun. "Maybe a bit better. I have to admit, it was a lot of fun."

Now wasn't the time to bring up what Vale had said about them not having body cameras yet. She already had a plan for that, which would benefit her staff while screwing him over. But that would have to wait 'til later, when there were fewer ears around.

Rebecca still hadn't forgotten it was the state police parking garage where the Yacht Club thugs had felt safe enough to ambush her and Hoyt. Or that it was in their evidence locker where Wallace's evidence had been tampered with enough to get cases tossed out of court. Which was why she always got copies and photographs from every case here, so if that happened to any of hers, she could track down what happened and where.

She glanced at Rhonda. "I understand you're only using our island as a place to transfer the bodies, right?"

Rhonda frowned, her eyebrows pulling down slightly. "Ye-es. Why?"

"I just wanted to make sure. That means you'll be taking the evidence from these two up north with you." She said it in a way to make sure Rhonda understood that this wasn't a question, but a suggestion. Almost a demand.

"I can. I didn't think you would want me to." Rhonda took a step closer and lowered her voice. "Is there something you're not telling me?"

Rebecca looked over at the troopers helping the divers unload the boat. They were the same ones who'd been standing around complaining the day before. "Maybe. I'll tell you later."

The special agent didn't turn but shifted slightly and side-eyed the men gathered around the boat. "Noted. We'll have a nice long chat later. Where you will give me all the details."

For now, Rebecca needed to have a look at what the two divers had brought in. They'd already shed their flippers and tanks. "I'd hoped to find them alive. To save them."

"When we didn't find them on any of the keys and didn't get reports from the beach towns, I was pretty sure this was how it would end." Rhonda tilted her head toward the boat where they were unloading the first body. "We'll be off-loading the second one momentarily."

The body was lifted out and set on the sand. Seaweed and other detritus speckled the corpse, adding streaks of red and green to the black-and-yellow marbled skin. A gaping hole took up the majority of the lower torso.

"That's not something a fish could do in such a short amount of time." Rebecca walked over and squatted down, inspecting the hole. The internal organs were gone, as she'd expected. It'd been more than twenty-four hours since Chester had warned them there were "two more," and from the looks of things, the first corpse had been in the water that entire time. The skin was loose and discolored. She glanced at his hands. Sure enough, a few fingers were missing as well. Half of the face was gone, including the nose, lips, and eyes.

"Looks like we'll have to check dental records."

Rhonda was already tapping away at a tablet. "I've got all the records for missing people ready to go so your M.E. can compare them."

"If this body went into the water at the same time as Able, he may not even be listed as missing yet." Rebecca stared at the teeth. They were easy enough to see, since most of the flesh that covered them had been eaten away already. Without touching the body, she leaned around, looking for any identifying marks. "Is that a tattoo?" She pointed to a section of leg still mostly intact.

Stepping around, Rhonda knelt beside the left leg. "Yup, that's a tattoo. Got a camera?" Not waiting for a response, she held up the tablet and snapped a few pictures herself.

Rebecca held her hand up to Hoyt, who was already clenching his lips tight. He passed over the camera gladly, and she duckwalked around, snapping close-up pictures as she went.

This caught the attention of several state troopers. A few of them even snickered. She would've ignored them, except she saw a face she recognized.

"Trooper Burke!" Rebecca waited 'til the man looked her

in the eyes. Just the sight of the incompetent, negligent, and possibly *corrupt* trooper tensed every muscle in her body. "Good to see you alive. When you abandoned your post at the Old Witch's Cottage, giving a serial killer the chance to kill another woman, we wondered if he'd killed you too. It's nice to see you're unharmed, unlike our headless victim. I talked to your senior about what could've pulled you away from your duties like that, but he never got back to me."

The group of staties split as all of them turned to look at Burke. Someone muttered, "Bitch," but she wasn't sure which one. And she didn't care.

"Yeah, really good to see your head's still attached." Rebecca stood and took a few steps toward the posse, her eyes locked on Burke's and her fists clenched so tightly her knuckles hurt. "You know that's what the killer did while you were AWOL. Chopped her head off. Flayed her skin so he could use it to decorate a book cover. Her remains looked so bad, it put the witness in the hospital. A teen girl with asthma."

She took another two steps forward as Burke's fellow troopers backed away from him. None of them wanted to be associated with a trooper who'd allowed such a thing to happen. She guessed Rhonda might be watching with disgusted interest while Hoyt was probably amused to the point of suppressing laughter. Not in the funny way either. He'd seen her tear into people before. Himself included.

And the victim had been his wife's friend.

"What time did you leave that night anyway? And before you left, did you happen to hear a woman screaming in pain or from terror? She was a real estate agent. Her father's only child. She was killed just across the marsh from where you were supposed to be stationed. Did you hear anything? See anything? I never did get a reason for what could have been so important as to pull you away. What was it? So I can add it to the official report."

"I..." His eyes darted around to the troopers he'd just been laughing with, who were all now scowling and shifting uncomfortably. Giving the locals grief was completely different from screwing up a case. That could be a career ender. "I got called out for a stranded motorist."

"A stranded motorist?" Rebecca took another step closer, and he took half a step back. "What time did that happen? Because the scene was clear at five that morning when you arrived. By eight thirty, there was a defiled, headless corpse set up on the building you were supposed to be watching. Did you happen to see a huge, hulking man drag Natalie Lamar's body there, then chop her head off and set it up to stare at her mutilated corpse?"

Burke gulped but tried to stay in place.

Rebecca took another step forward and felt someone move up behind her. She didn't look away from the man she was berating.

"I didn't see anything. I don't remember the time I got the call either. If I get a call, I respond. That's what we do. It's protocol."

"We also maintain crime scenes, especially when we suspect they'll be used again, Trooper Burke," Special Agent Lettinger said over Rebecca's shoulder. "Your dereliction of duty allowed a serial killer to remain on the loose. He killed another man the next day. Attacked a second, and nearly killed two law enforcement officers. The man you relieved that night ended up getting his head bashed in."

"She's the sheriff here!" Burke pointed a finger at Rebecca. "Why can't she maintain a force strong enough to police her own jurisdiction?"

"Is Virginia *not your jurisdiction*, Trooper?" Rebecca had never heard Rhonda yell before and was impressed with her lung capacity. "Get your ass off my crime scene! Head to your division headquarters. I'll be calling Captain Morgan to inform him of you and your sergeant's incompetence in this matter. You can expect to see him there as well."

Rhonda glared at the rest of the troopers, who'd put as much room between themselves and Burke as they could without running away.

"We are state troopers. This is *our* jurisdiction. Part of our job is to give support to the city and counties within our divisions as needed. If any of you cannot do the job, then feel free to resign." The special agent pointed at Burke's back as he made his way across the sand, heading for his cruiser. "Before you do that, say goodbye to Trooper Burke. I very much doubt any of you will see him at work again."

Rebecca grinned—she couldn't help it—and turned away from the troopers who were scattering now that the tongue-lashing was over. None of them wanted to even appear to have agreed with Burke, even if they had been not-so-subtly making digs at the weak sheriff's department.

They scrambled, four of them heading to the boat to help lift out the second body.

Rhonda and Rebecca watched them. A glint of light reflected off the second body's neck, and Rebecca walked over to see what it was. A gold chain necklace with a thick ring looped onto it had remained on the corpse's neck.

Rebecca studied the body. It appeared to be male, going by the tattered clothes. This one had a quarter-sized hole in the chest where a bullet had entered and a fist-sized hole in the back where it exited. Like the first one, the abdomen was eaten out, with all the soft organs gone. She could see straight through. Part of the face was left, loose and hanging from the cheekbones. One grayed-out blue eye stared at the sky.

"We got lucky with these, and the bigger scavengers

didn't sniff them out. I think I can see the bullet back there. I'll get a picture so I can zoom in on it."

She was in the middle of snapping pictures when Rhonda joined her.

Leaning over the body, the agent peered at the chest as well.

"Sheriff West?" Rhonda kept her eyes locked on the corpse. "About that talk? I think we need to have it now instead of later. This is going to end up being a federal case."

15

"Should we be worried about that?" Tweety asked.

The yacht we were on slid through the deep water like a sharp knife through Wagyu beef. I looked over to where one of my men was pointing. One of the state police boats that'd been patrolling the area earlier today was beached on the shore. A gaggle of cops stood around it. Most were dressed in the blue-gray uniforms of state troopers. They were clustered together, facing the local guys. It appeared they were having an argument with the sheriff and her men.

The sheriff was easy to spot. She was the short blond woman with...

Wait. There were two blond women standing on the beach. Neither was as tall as any of the men standing around. At this distance, it was hard to tell the height of any of them.

I picked up the binoculars to get a better look. One of the blonds was taller than the other and both wore bluish tops, but one wore the telltale black tie that marked her as part of the Virginia state police.

That meant the taller one was the sheriff. And she was the

one getting in the face of a tall trooper. I didn't know what she was saying, but he was backing up.

It only got worse when the trooper lady joined in with her. Two women yelling at one man, and the pussy was backing down. I snorted. They were so busy arguing among themselves that they weren't even paying attention to the crime scene they'd brought on shore.

Which was just how it was supposed to be. I wasn't going to admit to anyone that the increased presence of law enforcement officers made me uncomfortable. The fastest way to lose control of a crew was to show weakness. In front of them, I was confident and calm.

"Those bodies have been in the water long enough for the fish to clean up after us." I lowered the binoculars. "There's nothing to tie them to us. We took everything from their pockets before we dumped them."

"Except Chester. Chester's a problem." Chip spit, sending a stream of saliva over the railing.

Tweety shuffled around, watching the cops like they were cats and he was a little birdie about to be swallowed up. "But what if Chester wakes up?" He cracked his knuckles on the railing of the ship, leaning over the edge to keep watching as we curved around the island.

I laughed at that idea. "Oh, don't worry. He won't."

"How are we gonna make sure? He's in the hospital." Tweety turned and gaped at me. I wanted to smack his jaw shut just for being so stupid.

"Not sure if you know this, being the fucking new guy and all..." I rounded on him. He glanced down at his shoes. "But hospitals have doors. We can use them to walk through. Then we make sure Chester doesn't wake up. Do you know what we do after that?"

Tweety shook his head. "Uh..."

"We walk back out the door. It's just that easy."

Chip spoke up, flashing the broken tooth that'd earned him the name. "But what about all the extra cops around?"

"Don't worry about the cops." I raised the binoculars again.

The trooper who'd gotten the ass-chewing was storming off while the rest of them split up. The thin blue line was shattered, each of them going their own ways after the fight.

"We've got friends in high places. Friends we need to keep happy. I'm more worried about them. These cops are looking in the wrong direction. Let's head to the marina and dock. There're loose ends to tie up."

I shot them my most reassuring grin. Still, that many cops could be a nuisance. That was why I always made sure to keep an ace up my sleeve. And it was time to go visit him to make sure he was doing his job.

THE HOUSE WAS a piece of shit all shined up. All flash and no substance. I could always tell how recently a man had made his money by the way he kept his house, and how little he had. The phrase "money talks, but wealth whispers" was neatly showcased in this overly flashy house.

The neighborhood was blah. There were no gates, no privacy. Cars were parked in driveways so they could be shown off instead of protected inside garages. Wide windows with open curtains displayed what the nouveau riche had inside. These houses practically begged to be robbed.

This was a neighborhood where residents had to scream how much money they had, hoping their shrieking would hide their poor roots.

Rolling my eyes, I climbed out of my car. I had to step through water trickling down the driveway. The poor slob who lived here had actually washed his own car. Another way he could show off the solid black Tesla Model S he was overly proud of, I was sure.

Loud music blasted from his backyard, so I walked straight through. As expected, there wasn't even a fence, allowing me to just stroll, unobstructed, across emerald-green grass and up to a shed, right into his personal space.

My local contact was standing there, holding two pieces of wood while he used a framing hammer, of all things, to bash them together. The dents and chips were so bad, I could see them before I even stepped into the doorway.

"You trying to break that to bits or make something out of it?"

He actually jumped away from me, dropping his hammer.

I scooped it up, stepping into what I was sure he called his "man cave."

"Little trick. If you need to use force, use a piece of scrap to take the damage. That way, you're not screwing up your..." I examined the pieces of wood. "Birdhouse?"

"Yeah, uh..." He kept backing away, looking over my shoulder.

Was it to see if I was alone? Or to see if there was someone who could help him?

Staring him right in the eyes, I swung the hammer down, smashing the lumber he'd already marred up. "See? You don't want that to happen to something you're trying to show off." I glanced at the house behind me. "What are you looking at? Is your wife home?"

"Wife?" His voice broke, piping high with fear.

"That's fine." I turned back to him. He was halfway to the back wall now. "We're just two guys talking shop. Right?" I gestured to his pegboard hung with shiny tools.

"Yeah, talking shop." He smoothed down his shirt as if he were wearing an imaginary tie. "And how can I help you?"

"You know who I am? Who I work for?"

"I have an inkling. I assume you didn't come to my house on a weekend just for a chat."

"Of course I didn't." I lifted the framing hammer. Twirling it in my hands kept his attention on me. I hated when these guys pretended they were better than me. "I was just cruising around the island, and I couldn't help but notice there's an awful lot of badges around. Badges I was told you were supposed to be controlling."

The idiot actually looked confused. "I—"

"You *have* been keeping a close eye on them. Right?"

"Yes! Of course." He nodded, his eyes locked on the hammer. "Those are just some state cops who are parking their boats on our beach. That's all. We've already made arrangements with them so they won't interfere with business."

I slammed the hammer down again, making the wood and the idiot jump.

"See, that's where I have a problem." Pushing the wood aside, I rested my free hand on the worktable, leaning against it. "Cops in boats really cramp my style. They cramp *our* style. I can't have them out there getting in my way while I'm trying to work. If I can't work, I can't get paid. And if I don't get paid, I'm going to have to recoup my money some other way."

A car door slammed nearby, and I grinned. "Is that the missus? You've got a real pretty wife, right? Nice and young too? Real arm candy?" I pushed off the table and headed for the open workshop door. "I know plenty of people who'd pay top dollar for something like that."

"Wait!"

Slowing my steps, I swiveled back to look at him. "Yes?"

"I'll get the cops out of your area. There's no need to worry. Once the sun is down, they won't be out there."

"That's good. Real good. I have some business to conduct. If it goes well, you'll get your cut." I held up a finger to stop him from responding. "If it doesn't, you'll get cut."

"It'll be fine. I promise." He took several steps forward, finally finding his spine.

"It had better be. Because I already have one mess to clean up."

16

—————

Leaving Hoyt to babysit the scene, Rebecca drove back to the station with Rhonda following. She'd told the special agent to use her office for the phone call she needed to make. By the look of her, she was going to blow her lid any moment.

After checking with Viviane to see if there'd been any updates from the hospital about Chester Able's condition, then calling Justin Drake to make sure he'd gotten the bullet for ballistics tests, Rebecca went back to the break room to wait for Rhonda to finish her call.

"There you are." Rhonda stood in the doorway. "I didn't mean to keep you out of your office for so long."

Rebecca waved her off and motioned to the couch she was sitting on. "Don't worry about it. It's nice to relax back here every now and then. And it sounded like you had a lot of...displeasure to communicate."

Rhonda stood at the other end of the couch. "Displeasure. Yeah. You could say that. I knew the troops down here weren't as, let's say, *invested* as my guys, but what I saw today had me fuming. *Has* me fuming. Captain Morgan oversees all these troopers, and he'll be made aware of this. I'm going to ask him to see what's going on at that station."

"How well do you know this captain?" While it had been the sergeant she'd had so many issues with, she'd never spoken with the captain about him.

"I know him. He's a standup guy, someone I trust. He'll dig into this and see if there's anything underlying the actions of Burke or his sergeant. You know, we still need to talk. Did you notice what that second body was wearing?"

Rebecca pulled her camera out and opened the pictures she'd taken before they left. "A necklace of some kind? Gold, I think."

"And a ring." Rhonda slid around to peer over her shoulder. "There. That ring. Does that look familiar to you?"

Zooming in, Rebecca peered at the piece. It was a thick ring, clearly a man's, with a design in the center that looked like a crest. Three stars laid diagonally within two bars. "Not really. Does it to you?"

Rhonda pressed her lips tight and nodded. "That's the Overbay family ring. That's their family crest."

Overbay? That name sounded familiar. Rebecca sighed and closed her eyes, hoping her memory was wrong. "Senator Paul Overbay? U.S. senator for Virginia?"

"That's the one. His son, Frederick, went missing a few days ago. He was supposed to be out on a boating trip, but his boat never came back."

"A senator's son goes missing on a boating trip. Then I'm graced with two unidentified corpses and a seriously wounded victim on my shore. And one of the corpses has a ring with the family crest of Virginia's U.S. senator on him." Rebecca's words were muffled as she rested her face in her hands. "So I guess until we get a positive ID, we'll operate under the assumption this is Overbay's missing son. And we can try to determine if he went boating with a known drug dealer."

Why can't cases just be easy?

"Until we get something to link them, there's nothing to say they were together, though." Rhonda's words made Rebecca chuckle.

"Or that Able isn't the one who killed the Overbay kid. Or the other one."

"Don't you just love it when things get even more complicated the more evidence you accumulate?"

Rebecca lifted her face from her hands and patted Rhonda on the shoulder. "Sounds like you have a lot of work to do. Do be careful. Dealing with congressional critters is a good way to tank your career."

"That's why I like to foist it onto the FBI when I can. They're always good at doing detailed searches for my cases." Rhonda winked at her. "Or someone who's had their training, at least."

Holding her hands up, Rebecca leaned away. "Hey, that's your missing persons case. I've just got a shooting victim. Like you said at the beach, those are your bodies."

Rhonda chuckled. "No, *you* said they were my bodies. But it's fine. The Feds don't want the case. They just want to help so they can see what's happening with it. Win-win for me." Her eyes gleamed, and Rebecca knew something else was coming. "As you know, Overbay was shot in the sternum. Did you notice the hole it made and the shards in his back, indicating it was from a high-velocity firearm instead of, say, a Glock or a knife or a screwdriver?"

Rebecca shifted the picture down to view the chest. "I did. And the bullet is still in the back ribs."

"Once we compare ballistics on that," Rhonda tapped the screen, "to the one pulled from Able's arm, we'll know if they were shot by the same gun."

Rebecca's radio chirped to life. "Hey, Boss?"

"Yeah, Viviane?"

"Hospital called with an update. They said Able is stable now."

Rhonda's eyebrows went up. "Sounds like it's time to go talk to your victim. I'll go to the M.E. with the bodies and see if that really is Overbay we found. After all," she shrugged, "it's just a ring. Not a DNA match."

Rebecca rose to her feet and led the way out of the break room. "Yeah, but neither of us believes that."

"Of course not. Neither of us is that lucky."

17

"What are you doing back here? I thought you were watching the scene at the beach."

Hoyt looked up from his computer as Darian walked into the bullpen. He was still in his civvy clothes but was carrying the garment bag he used for his uniform.

"I was just babysitting the scene for the agent from Norfolk while she made some phone calls and talked with the boss."

"Oh, yeah? Didn't she have enough of her own guys there..." He trailed off as Hoyt started smirking. "What? Did I miss something?"

"Looks like we might end up sharing this case with the staties. But go get changed. This is going to take too long to explain." Darian nodded and took a step toward the locker room. "Wait. How was group?" Every other Sunday morning, Darian headed to the mainland to meet up with a group of vets. Hoyt was never sure if it was group therapy or some bonding type of thing.

"Good. I mean, ya know. There was a lot of bitching, some

griping. Really bad coffee, so it felt like we were really back together in the service. But," he ran his hand over his chin, "yeah, it was good stuff. It's good to see breakthroughs. Ya know?"

"Uh, yeah. Sounds good." Hoyt did not know. He also didn't think it was his place to ask. One thing he did know about veteran groups—those who didn't know never would. There was no way a man who had never enlisted, let alone been deployed, could understand what those people went through. He just wanted to support his friend. That was why he always checked in with him once he got back from a meeting.

And Darian knew that too. He gave him a grin and a nod and went to get changed into his uniform.

Hoyt went back to reading through the missing persons file while he waited. He got to the end of it and looked up, noticing that Darian wasn't back yet, and chuckled to himself. The younger deputy was probably back there primping, making sure his uniform was all straight and proper, lining up his buttons with his fly and all that jazz. Seeing an update notification on the case file, he opened it and saw everything Rebecca had added to the folder.

"Okay!" Darian clapped his hands together loudly as he came back and walked past Hoyt to get his own cup. "Fill me in while I get coffee made from beans and not whatever that pig shit was at the VA."

Another sure sign Darian had spent time hanging out with other soldiers, his language became a lot coarser.

"You might want to brace yourself for this." Hoyt spun his chair around so he could witness Darian's reaction. "One of the bodies they pulled up today…we think it was Senator Overbay's missing son."

"You're shitting me." Darian looked over as he was pouring his coffee, then spluttered into a hodge-podge of curses as he missed his cup and soaked his hand with the hot liquid.

Hoyt laughed. "I told you to brace yourself, dipshit."

Darian shook his hand, then ran it under cold water. "A senator's son? Glad that's not technically one of our cases."

"Unless ballistics links him to our guy."

"Oh, shit." Darian sipped his coffee and leaned over Hoyt's shoulder to read his screen. "Do we have a match?"

"Not yet. But two of them had bullets stuck in them. One guy didn't. At least, we didn't see it on the scene. Waiting on Dr. Flynn to get the second one out so we can compare it to the first." Hoyt pulled up the pictures from the scene Rebecca had uploaded from her camera.

"Oh, this one is getting juicy." Darian turned away to his own desk. "Not in a good way. The same way a latrine gets juicy."

Hoyt eyed the cup of coffee he'd been about to pick up and slid it away. "Nice imagery."

"What are we doing, then?" Keys clacked as Darian signed on to his computer.

"We're looking for connections between Able and Fred-erick Overbay."

"Fred-er-ick." Darian twisted his mouth around as he pronounced the name. "Who names their kid that these days?"

"The kind of people who have a family crest, a seat in the senate, can trace their roots back to someone who had a seat in Parliament, and give their kids signet rings so we can easily identify them when they wash ashore with a bunch of other junkies."

Darian snorted. "These are the people who decide when and where we go to war too. Everything makes so much more sense now. Fred-er-rick. I need to remember this one for the next meeting."

"Let's get this case settled first. That way, they can read about it in the paper too."

"Another upside to the staties taking over..."

At that pause, Hoyt looked over at Darian, who was grinning over his cup. Whatever he had lined up was not going to be good. He knew it in his bones.

"What's that?"

"You don't have to stand in at any autopsies for this one." He tipped his coffee at Hoyt in a *cheers* gesture.

Hoyt turned back to his work. He had to admit, Darian was right. That was one silver lining in this whole shit sandwich.

18

Though there'd been more traffic on the bridge than I'd hoped, the trip to the mainland had been uneventful. I honestly couldn't fathom how people dealt with that crush of tourists on a daily basis. But I was hoping the crowds would work to my advantage.

Coastal Ridge's midsize building, which served as the hospital for the region, had its pros and cons where my plan was concerned. It could serve a fair number of patients, which meant it should be busy enough to blend in with other visitors and go unnoticed. But there was also a small-town vibe, which meant everyone knew everyone.

Although there was a parking garage next door that served several facilities, I easily spotted the sheriff's SUV parallel parked on the street out front.

I took a trip around the building, just to scope it out. It seemed standard in design, with rooms on the outside wall and inner walls. Hallways connected all the rooms to the nurses' stations, which were spaced out at either end of the building. Of course, I could only see so much from my location on the street.

If this hospital was like every other I'd ever been in, there were plenty of places to move unseen. Areas of the building the sheriff wouldn't go because they were intended for employees only. Places I could get through.

It was a Sunday afternoon. One of the slowest days for emergency staff, and a day when they weren't taking appointments. Now was the perfect time to strike. I'd just have to slip around the sheriff. She and I wanted to talk to the same person, after all.

In the back of the building, I found what I was looking for. The employees' entrance. A simple black metal door with just a handle and a card reader. That was easy enough to bypass. A quick look around showed no one watching. There weren't even any cameras mounted by this entrance.

Like all commercial buildings, there was a thick row of neatly pruned hedges surrounding it. I snapped a branch off and easily stripped it of twigs and leaves, dumping them on the grass so they wouldn't be seen. Once I had the right length, I propped the branch up against the door, making sure it was just slightly leaning into the seam where the door met the frame.

Keeping an eye on it, I slammed my fist into the door, making a ruckus loud enough to be heard inside. Checking one last time and having to move fast, I made sure the coast was clear and ducked behind the bushes by the door. I was tucked back far out of view when the door slammed open.

A nurse I presumed, who looked like the epitome of a man who would argue with the manager over the slightest infraction, opened the door and glared back and forth, scanning for whoever'd been knocking like a maniac. He was so focused on finding someone to scream at, he never even noticed the trimmed branch that fell into the frame and kept the door from locking when he turned with a huff and went back inside.

He never walked past the windows I was crouched below, making me certain there was another door just inside. Giving him enough time to create some distance, I slipped up to the door and slowly opened it. I couldn't hear anything, so I straightened and walked through like I had every right to be there, kicking the branch out of the way.

Climbing the stairs to the patient floors, I entered the hallway. As expected, it stretched left and right with doors dotted along both walls. In front of me, a smaller hallway intersected my path. The quiet voices of two women came from one direction, but they were out of sight, their words indistinct. A plaque on the wall showed I was on the nonemergency side of the building.

Stepping silently, I made my way down the smaller hallway. The voices came from the second intersection, not the first one, where a rolling cart loaded with covered food trays had been left. Closer now, I looked left and right. Those doors were numbered only. Patient rooms, not clinics or offices.

Looking down at the food trolley, I read the paperwork on top of it. Only a few lines down the page, I found the meal intended for Chester Able. Room 203.

In the hallway, I could see even-numbered rooms on the right. Which meant the room I needed was on the left.

Taking the food tray marked for Chester Able, I crossed to a door on that side. The narrow window showed no one in the room. I twisted the doorknob, slipped inside, and set it firmly closed before I let go. It looked like a consultation room, with a table along one wall and the typical sink and cupboards.

Though I ransacked the cupboards, I found nothing of value. But a cart in the corner of the room held what I needed—a stash of dirty scrubs headed for the laundry. I didn't care if I had someone else's DNA on my disguise. Perhaps it would even help conceal my own.

I made quick work, flipping through the collection of soiled scrubs before finding one close to my size. People saw what they expected to see. A man wearing scrubs would fade into the background in a hospital, which was just what I needed to do. There was nothing to hide the scar across my forehead, though, so I'd have to deal with that. A hat would draw unwanted attention.

My plan was to remain inconspicuous. But if someone got in my way, I wouldn't hesitate to put them down. I had a job to do. It was either get it done or get dead. The cartel wasn't forgiving of failure.

Pulling my knife, I cut a slit in my scrubs just above the shirt pocket and double-checked that I could reach the syringe through the opening. Each room I'd peeked into had a spare box of gloves by the door, and this one was no exception, so I pulled a pair on.

Everything settled and ready, I picked up Able's food tray, held my head high, and walked through the door to go have a little conversation with him before sending him to Hell.

19

"You got here fast."

"That's the joy of the flashing lights. It means I can drive whatever speed I want." Rebecca grinned at Dr. Amanda Stuard, Chester Able's attending physician. For a moment, she worried she'd overstepped with the joke when the doctor's forehead creased. Rebecca hadn't met the woman beyond a phone call, when she'd arranged to come to the mainland to interview her victim.

An uncomfortable silence followed as the doctor shuffled some papers on the counter. Dr. Stuard's graying hair was barely concealed by a box of off-the-shelf, sandy-brown hair dye. Going by the neon-green resin clogs she wore, it was clear the doctor was someone who spent more time on her feet than she wanted.

She turned to face Rebecca, then broke into a broad smile. "My apologies. I happened to see Dr. Flynn in the hallway after speaking with you and she asked me to, and I quote, 'bust your balls.' I assume you two are friends and that I haven't just made a terrible first impression."

Rebecca smiled back. "Ah, say no more. Yes, Bailey and I

like to share friendly banter. Usually, we direct it at others. Now I know how it feels to be on the receiving end."

"Goodness, I'll have to stay on my toes now, won't I?"

"It's probably a good idea."

Dr. Stuard's smile was fleeting as she returned to her professional persona. "We can head to Mr. Able's room. It's that one over there. Room 203."

"So how is Able doing? He made it through the surgery well?"

"Recovering nicely. He's back in his room."

When Rebecca looked over a nurse's shoulder in that direction, a staff member in green scrubs was picking up a lunch tray with his hands in gloves.

Something seemed off.

She did a quick check of the nurse in front of her, then of two of the staff passing by, then the lunch tray guy again. Everyone had their ID badge but him. She glanced at the doctor's white lab coat—ID badge. "Does everyone who works here have to wear a badge on a lanyard around their neck?"

The doctor's head turned in the direction Rebecca gestured. "What? Yes, of course. Why?" She scanned the area around the nurses' station. "Did you see someone without one?"

Alarm bells rang in Rebecca's head as the guy in scrubs slipped out of sight into room 203 with his lunch tray. Her hand jerked to her Springfield Armory 1911. She hadn't gotten a glimpse of his whole face, but she could've sworn she saw a jagged scar above an eyebrow. Just like Locke had said about the man at the beach. "Yes, and he just went into Able's room."

A door on the other side of the hallway opened. A tall nurse named Ethan, who Rebecca recognized from previous visits to the hospital, popped his head out the door.

"Hey, Doc, did you take room 203's food? I left it on the trolley, then went to get his water, and now it's gone."

Rebecca reached for Dr. Stuard with her left hand, unsnapped her holster with her right, and had just opened her mouth when the door to room 203 opened.

When the man in green scrubs stepped out, he started to turn toward them. If Rebecca hadn't been on high alert, she might've missed his hesitation as he noticed Ethan and turned to the right instead, away from them all. His right arm was out of view, but she'd swear he was reaching inside his unusually bulky scrubs.

No ID badge. Definitely has a scar. He's wearing street clothes under his scrubs. And those shoes. No one who spent long hours on their feet would ever wear bendable running shoes with no support.

"No. I—"

"You, in the green scrubs!" Rebecca pulled the doctor behind her. "Stop where you are!"

He spun, drawing a gun. Rebecca caught a flash of a serious, drawn face. A deep, crooked scar cut across his forehead, puckering his hairline. She looked him straight in the eye even as she dropped low, dragging Stuard down with her.

After his sudden dodge and pivot coming out the door, the man's aim was off. Now he had to shift to his left to avoid hitting the wall. The shot went wide and high, well over the heads of Rebecca and Dr. Stuard. Then he was running down the hallway.

"Get down!" Rebecca tried to shove Dr. Stuard behind the counter, but the woman twisted, crouched, and bolted for Able's room to check on her patient.

Rebecca ran ahead of her, gun drawn. "Lock the doors and stay down!"

The hallway wasn't very long, and the shooter made it into the stairwell before she could get a safe shot off.

"Ethan!" Dr. Stuard yelled. "Get in here!"

Rebecca twitched from the doctor's shrieking cry as she approached the door to the stairs.

She pulled her radio as she ran. "Shots fired at Coastal Ridge Hospital. Notify their PD. Send units. Sheriff in pursuit on foot." She held her breath and heard the shooter's heavy footsteps echoing from down the stairs. Staying pressed against the stairwell wall, she swiveled her arms to the left, keeping her gun ahead of her, ready to fire.

There was no one to shoot at. As she exited the stairwell on the main floor, a sliding shadow on the floor and walls showed where an automatic glass door was closing. She put on a burst of speed, not sure if the door had simply been triggered as he passed or if the man had left the building.

Until the man, now wearing a white coat, left the ambulance bay and crossed the parking lot, heading for the shopping center next door.

"Stop!"

Rebecca wasn't sure who'd yelled as she twisted to get through. The closing door hit the toe of her shoe and she tripped, stumbling across the sidewalk. Even then, she kept her gaze locked on the man. Throwing herself forward, she tried to right herself and continue the chase.

A strong grip on her shirt snatched her backward as the roar of an approaching box truck finally registered. Her foot slid off the curb as she fell on her ass. The scream of tires drifting in front of her made her jerk her leg out of the way.

"Are you okay?"

Rebecca looked up at the person who'd saved her from getting hit. A woman in scrubs was staring down at her with wide eyes. She wore a hospital-issued ID badge hanging from a logoed lanyard, indicating her name was Elizabeth Hart.

"Damn, didn't your mother teach you to look both ways before you cross the street?"

Rebecca ignored the question and lifted her radio. "Dispatch, suspect heading west toward shopping center. Get Coastal Ridge PD here ASAP. Over."

"Suspect?" The stranger glanced up, but the truck was still in front of them, blocking their view. "What's going on?"

Rebecca swiped a bead of sweat from her temple. "It's a long story." Then she was running again.

20

Rebecca turned a circle in the middle of the parking lot. Though she was surrounded by cruisers from three different stations, she continued to look for the man. She'd been forced to go back to Able's room to keep him safe while the doctor dealt with what she said was likely an overdose of potassium. Dr. Stuard had gotten him stabilized without much issue.

Once the VSP had descended, she'd left them with guard duty so she could help with the search.

"What about the bank over there?" She turned to Rhonda, who was sitting in her cruiser, coordinating her officers.

"I've already got my people pulling it." Rhonda tapped her screen a few times, then frowned. "My people went through the hospital's security footage and there was no way to ID the guy. The angles were terrible. About the only useful piece of info was the direction he headed. Though he could always circle back, I concentrated our efforts on the direction he fled."

Sighing with frustration, Rebecca gave up on watching

every man who crossed into her view. It'd been almost an hour since the incident. He had to be long gone. Or he was hidden so well they weren't going to find him.

"Did you happen to notice the hurricane that came through here a couple weeks back?" She waved her hands at the stumps of trees. "Coastal Ridge didn't get hit as hard as the island, but they still suffered damage."

"You guys really can't catch a break, can you?" Rhonda leaned out of the car, shielding her eyes to look over.

"Not when I spend half my time cleaning up someone else's messes and the other half trying to remove the cancer that's settled into the island."

"Cancer?"

Rebecca leaned against the hood of her cruiser. There was no one else around. They were on a nearly abandoned street whose traffic had been diverted while the area was canvassed.

"I've walked into something, Rhonda. It's the reason I'm sheriff now."

Rhonda slid her laptop and tablet off her lap, climbing out of the car to come stand next to her. "What do you mean? Walked into what?"

Rebecca crossed her arms. "There aren't just drug dealers sailing past our island."

"You mean the human traffickers you caught?" Rhonda glanced around them, catching on to how uneasy Rebecca was.

"Them too. I think they're all part of something bigger. The residents of the island aren't getting the justice they deserve. I don't like speaking ill of the dead, but the last sheriff turned a blind eye to a lot of things." She hunched her shoulders a bit more, leaning forward.

"That's always the problem with tourist towns." Rhonda

groaned, leaning on the cruiser next to Rebecca. "Money talks, and crime chases away the tourists. If you don't admit there's a crime, then it's easy to play idyllic beach vacation spot."

Rebecca frowned down at the other woman. "You seem to have caught on to this way too fast."

Rhonda sighed. "I wish this was the first time I've run into something like this. But it's not. Norfolk, Virginia Beach, and Hampton PDs are also really bad about this."

"Do they also have a group of rich bastards throwing parties with underage girls and lots of drugs?"

"Yeah, they've got the largest naval station in the continental U.S." Rhonda's sardonic grin caused Rebecca to laugh in response. Sometimes, it was the only thing to do when the truth was so bleak. "Really, though, we do. Not sure if they're organized or anything, but…"

"They are."

Rhonda turned to her. "How do you know that?"

"Simple. You've got some of my girls up there too. They're picked up here, then, once they're trained, tested, proven loyal enough, whatever you want to call it, they get moved up to Norfolk. I don't know where they go from there."

"Because they're loyal at that point, making money, and move on pretty quickly?" It was a question, but they both knew it was true. "Do you have names?"

Rebecca thought about the stacks of papers, filled with names she kept in three separate, secure locations, including with her lawyer in case of her death.

"Not yet, but I'm putting them together. And that's just the start of it."

It wasn't just her life on the line if she was wrong to trust Rhonda. It was Hoyt, Darian, Viviane, and possibly Locke too. It was Justin, who was currently working their latest crime scene and collecting evidence. It was also Robert Leigh, the man who'd led her to that list and who was currently locked up in the criminal psych ward of a hospital in Norfolk.

Rhonda didn't look at her, simply shrugging her shoulders. "Well, when you want to start pulling them down, I'll do all I can to help you."

"I do have one name." Rebecca couldn't help herself. She'd tried to make a difference, to save a life before it got too twisted. "A victim."

"You want me to keep an eye out for her? Keep her safe if I can?"

She nodded. "Serenity McCreedy. She was seventeen in June. I can't remember when her birthday is. I do remember her boyfriend, Chris, is thirty something. She was an assault victim here. The same man who killed her friend tried to kill her because she knew about their affair."

"I'll keep an eye out. Obviously, I can't promise anything."

"Obviously. I mean, I had her in my custody. Held her while she cried. Then I went to take her victim testimony, and she was gone. I haven't heard from her since. I just fear her name is going to end up on your missing persons list one day soon."

"Your man is coming back. And he's not empty-handed." Rhonda nodded, warning Rebecca that their moment of secure talking was over.

Rebecca looked where she nodded. Hoyt was walking out of the lot at the edge of the shopping center carrying an overstuffed bag. "Frost is a good man. So is Hudson." She straightened to go meet him and see what he'd found.

"What about Locke?"

And that was the million-dollar question. "Jury's still out on that one."

"Noted." Rhonda once again moved up next to her and

kept her voice low. "I've got some favors owed to me. I can check into your man, Locke. See if there's anything to see, at least."

With Hoyt's hair soaked in sweat, the gray really stood out. He had that slight hunch he'd developed every time he overdid things and irritated his appendix surgery scar.

Darian pushed his way out of the brush, laughing with one of the troopers he'd gone out to search with. The man could make friends wherever he went.

Rebecca thought back to the black eye and bloody lip Locke had been sporting recently.

"I'd appreciate that. I want to make sure none of my guys get into trouble because we trusted people we shouldn't have."

"Found it, Boss. It's a set of green scrubs and a white lab coat. Was this what he was wearing?" Hoyt came to a halt in front of her, opening the bag and breathing heavily in the hot, thick air.

"Yeah, looks like it. Head inside and find Dr. Stuard. Verify with her these are theirs. Then have Justin take them. Enjoy the air-conditioning while you can. After that, I'm going to need you to hold down the fort for me."

Rebecca's phone buzzed, and she pulled it out of her pocket to check it. She didn't even need to read the message, as the contact name was enough to let her know things had just taken another turn. "You already called Senator Overbay and told him what you found?"

"Yeah. Why?" It would've been easy enough for Rhonda to lean over and see the screen, but she didn't push.

"Because the FBI is texting me. My old partner, Special Agent Benji Huang. Looks like I need to grab my go bag."

Her phone buzzed again as another message came through, and she started typing a response.

Darian wiped the sweat off his nose with his thumb. "Something else come up?"

"I've been summoned to the Capitol to have a chat with a senator."

21

Rebecca dropped the armful of laundry she'd just pulled from the dryer onto the kitchen table as a knock sounded at the door. Playing things safe, she unsnapped her holster before moving to answer it.

"Who is it?" She stood to the left of the door, ready for anything, her gun half drawn.

"It's me, babe. I heard you got off early."

Hearing Ryker's voice had her smiling, and she quickly resecured her 1911. Opening the door, she reached out and pulled him into a kiss. "I haven't gotten off yet. But maybe if you help?"

"Well, I am a handyman." Ryker stepped through the door, walking her back as his hands slid around her waist. They stopped when he reached her holster. "You're still armed? Oh. You're really not off duty yet, are you?"

She sighed and turned away, motioning to the pile of clothes on the table.

He laughed and closed the door behind him, locking it as she'd insisted he always do. "It's good to be the boss, isn't it? You can pop home during the day to get some chores done. I know I like nothing better than to come home in the middle of my shift to fold laundry." He stepped farther into the house and spotted her bag on the table next to the pile with her toiletry kit, already packed and ready to go. "Um, what's going on here?"

For a brief moment, Rebecca saw a spark of fear in his eyes. He looked at her, and her heart melted a little. "Don't worry. It's just a one-night trip. Two, tops. Depending on flights and schedules."

"Does this have anything to do with what happened at the hospital on the mainland?" His eyes jumped between her packing and her face, searching.

She walked around the table, grabbing the bits and pieces she needed, and started rolling them into tight tubes she could easily pack in her carry-on bag. "Actually, no. It has to do with someone the VSP pulled from the water."

He frowned but a bit of the worry left his eyes. "I didn't hear about that."

Rebecca sighed and dug around, looking for her other sock. "You can't tell anyone yet. We just got the confirmation ourselves. Rhonda, the VSP agent I've been working with, got a rush put on the dental match. A senator's son was picked up by divers. He'd been shot. And it looks like his death is connected to the man we found alive on the beach Saturday."

"Was he connected to what happened at the hospital, then?"

"Maybe." She shrugged, watching him as the skin around his eyes kept twitching like he was in pain. "He was trying to kill the survivor. Put a lethal dose of potassium into his IV, but his doctor, Dr. Stuard, was able to save him. She saw the syringe and yanked his line, so he didn't even get the full amount, and she got it all sorted out. She moved fast for someone wearing clogs. She even ran toward the shooter to get to her patient. Can you believe that?"

"Wow. That's impressive, and kind of fearless. She sounds more like a firefighter rushing into harm's way than a physician in a small-town hospital." He shook his head. "I thought there was a shooting. But you said he used a syringe?"

"He did. When I noticed him, he pulled a gun and got a shot off while running."

His frown was back and stronger than ever.

Rebecca took his hands. "It's okay. It wasn't even pointed at us. He was contorting as he exited Able's room and ended up shooting the ceiling. And a nice nurse named Elizabeth stopped me from getting hit."

"Hit? Like in a fistfight?"

"No. Not a fight. From the truck I almost ran in front of."

Ryker took a slow, deep breath and stared at her with hooded eyes. Then he pulled out a dining room chair and sat at the table. "Okay. I'm going to need you to explain this all to me, starting at the beginning."

Laughing at herself and how poorly she'd explained things, Rebecca started all over again, this time going in order. By the time she was done, her bag was packed and ready to go. She dropped the rest of the laundry in the basket to deal with later.

"And now you're going to D.C. to inform Senator Overbay about his son's death?"

She wobbled her head back and forth. "No. He knows about the confirmation. His son's dental records were in the system since he was a missing person."

"Then why are you going?" He took her hands in his. "And why do you look so worried about it?"

"Me?" Rebecca was surprised by that question. She'd been trying to reassure him, and he was worried about her?

"Yes, you. You look anxious as hell." He stroked her lower

lip with his thumb, and she realized she'd been biting it the whole time.

She pursed her lips and blew out the breath she'd been holding. "'Cause I don't want to go to D.C. I'm not looking forward to dealing with the traffic and the headache of flying into Reagan. I don't want to deal with senators, their staff, or the security checkpoints you have to go through to get to them. And I don't want to be reminded of why I left."

"You know," he scooted forward, still holding her hands, "you never actually told me why you left. Just that you wanted to come here afterward because you had such fond memories of the island."

Rebecca blinked at him. He was right. "It was because of another senator, actually. I didn't know at the time, but he was involved in the murder of my parents. It's a long story."

Ryker leaned back in his chair. "I've got nowhere to be tonight. Do you?"

She nodded and poked her bag. "I'm taking the red-eye. Need to be at the airport by midnight."

"Midnight?"

"When you fly on the state's dime, you get the cheapest flight. And the one with the totally random layover in Newark that takes nearly four hours instead."

Ryker stood and walked over to the police scanner she kept turned on when she wasn't at work and wasn't sleeping. "You're already packed. We have six hours before you have to leave. I'll order a pizza. And you can explain it all to me." He leaned over and kissed the top of her head. "That way, before you get on the plane to take you back, you can unload some of that burden and not take it with you."

He started to turn away, but Rebecca caught his belt loop and pulled him close, wrapping her arms around his butt and resting her head on his hip.

"Strangely, that sounds delightful."

22

As the plane landed, the sun rose, and Rebecca kept her eyes locked on the view of the Potomac River, steam wafting off it in the morning light. It was one of the best views of the area, or, at least, the one that had the fewest bad memories attached to it.

Her flight arrived on time, which was surprising. Not having any checked bags and with it being so early, she got through the only couple hundred travelers moving through the airport and outside into the cool morning without issue. A few dozen other people had flown into the Capitol to start their week, and these crowded the sidewalk as she struggled to reach the pick-up area.

After she'd received only a cryptic message from her former partner, Rebecca's mind had been racing about the purpose of the visit. Clearly, it had something to do with the senator's deceased son. But she hadn't worked out why Benji was involved or why she needed to take a red-eye flight to D.C.

The good memories she had of this city, like the National Mall where she and Calvin had gone walking after their first date, were now soured by the events that had led to her leaving. But the roads that took her to her dream job every morning before she was forced to resign, and the paths she jogged to keep in shape before being shot, and even the heavy morning traffic…those brought nice memories.

So maybe there was a bit of a silver lining.

A horn honked nearby, followed by someone calling her name.

Ducking low, Rebecca peered at the heavily tinted passenger window of a black sedan as it rolled down, showing the interior. Benjirou "Benji" Huang waved at her from behind the steering wheel, his dark eyes hidden behind the Ray-Bans he was notorious for. Pulling her bag from her shoulder, she opened the door and climbed in, dropping it onto the back floorboard.

Benji was already slipping into traffic before she'd managed to get her seat belt on. She didn't ask him anything or attempt a conversation as he maneuvered through the heavy congestion until he was safely on the interstate. The amiable silence they'd developed as partners in the FBI now felt oppressive, and Rebecca finally punctured the stillness.

"Okay, Benji, spill it. What's the real reason I'm here?" Rebecca turned away from the not-so-glorious view of the taillights in front of them and stared at him. His face was just as mirror smooth as ever. Every black hair was perfectly in place.

"Because I was nice enough to wake up stupid early to come and pick you up, so you didn't have to deal with finding a taxi."

While that part was true, he had not brought coffee. Rebecca figured she didn't owe him anything.

"We both know that's not what I'm asking about and you're dodging the question. And that if it hadn't been you who contacted me yesterday, if anyone else from the FBI or

Overbay's staff had called me, there was no way I would've gotten on a plane at midnight to fly out here for this meeting. So who pulled strings and what did they tell you to get me up here?"

He glanced over at her. "Real talk? This early in the morning?"

"Of course. I'm about to go to my appointment with a senator and I want to be prepared." She twisted in her seat and crossed her arms, waiting for him to answer. After working side by side with him for years, she could already tell this was going to be a complicated tale.

"The associate deputy director came down with Overbay and read me in on an incident that was connected with the disappearance of Overbay's son." He tipped his glasses down so she could see his eyes, letting her know in his own way that he wasn't hiding anything from her, before returning his gaze to the road. "He came to us personally with this information."

That was surprising. It had to be something serious if a senator took the time to bring it to their attention himself instead of sending an aide to deal with it. "What information did he have? And what was the event?"

"Senator Overbay was being blackmailed."

That did not surprise Rebecca, not after all her time working in the FBI. "So is it a dead body, drugs, bribery, or a secret sex scandal?" Those were the most common things that could tank a politician's career.

"There were some drugs involved and now he's dead, according to your investigation."

"Mine? It was about his son?"

"Something his son did, yeah. And it was caught on video. His son was definitely in over his head. I'm not the one he asked for, so I'm not sure what he was doing that was black-mail worthy. I was never allowed to see the video. But I do know that the senator was told to pay up and not run for office again, or the video would be released during the midterm elections."

Rebecca rolled her eyes. "So once his son was dead, and the news couldn't hurt him and would only help him with sympathy votes, he told the FBI about it."

Benji shook his head. "I know you're not going to believe this, but it's true. Senator Overbay brought us the tape at the same time he reported that his son was missing. He brought it to us in the hopes it would help find his son." He raised his perfectly plucked eyebrows. "The man is a unicorn, Rebecca. A senator who doesn't care about losing his seat if it would help his son."

That was surprising. Rebecca straightened in her seat, keeping an eye out for the road signs to see how much longer it would be until they reached the Capitol Building. "Did he agree to pay up?"

Benji shrugged, his thin shoulders moving easily in his tailored suit jacket. "I'm not sure. But I can tell you the video hasn't been released to the media yet."

"So no one knows what's on it?"

"No one but the blackmailers and the senator, as far as I know. I was only provided a very high-level read-in on the subject matter, but almost no specifics. Also he asked for you by name as soon as he was told his son had died. He called us still crying."

Rebecca frowned. A senator she'd never met, never worked with or for, and he'd asked for her by name. Whatever put her on his radar could not be a good thing.

It never was in this city.

23

The sun was just peeking over the horizon, stretching the shadows as Hoyt pulled his keys out to unlock the station door. The crisp *thunk* of the dead bolt echoed down the empty street. Golden light glinted off the star on the glass door so brightly, he had to squint to see.

Stepping inside, he set his travel mug on the windowsill so he could lock up behind him. It was another thirty minutes before he had to open for the day, and he wanted to spend that time getting the office ready and let the air-conditioning cool down after adjusting the temperature.

He never liked having to cover for the sheriff. And he downright hated it when he had to cover in the middle of a complicated case that crossed jurisdictions like this one did. Rebecca had a good rapport with Rhonda, but he barely knew her. Although he knew his colleagues in Coastal Ridge, the incident at the hospital created yet another jurisdictional layer.

"Deputy Frost."

He jumped and reached for his gun before he recognized

the voice coming from behind him—a voice that did not belong inside the locked building.

Turning away from the door, he laid eyes on Richmond Vale standing behind the dispatch counter.

"Rich. What are you doing in here?" Hoyt looked around, checking if anyone else unauthorized was inside. He, of course, had a key to get in. So did Melody and Viviane and Rebecca, naturally. But there shouldn't have been any other wandering station keys. "How did you get in here?"

Vale ignored his questions completely, even waved them away, as if they were annoying little gnats. "I wanted a chance to speak to you personally. You've served this county and our town for quite a long time now. I thought you deserved to hear this before anyone else."

He stepped up to the half door. Hoyt narrowed his eyes as Vale passed through into the lobby as if he did so all the time. There was supposed to be only one magnetic fob that unlocked the door to the bullpen, and that stayed with the sheriff's keys. So Vale had to have one on him too.

Rebecca had warned him about things like this. Hell, she'd even given him a recorder and downloaded an app for it on his phone—for situations such as this one. But he hadn't figured out how to set his to a specific motion like she'd done on her phone. Fiddling with it now would be way too obvious. He'd have to rely on the security cameras.

"Whatever you need to tell me, you can say during office hours." *And around other witnesses.* He knew Vale wouldn't be having this talk with him if Viviane were around to hear it.

"Not this. I really shouldn't be doing this since it isn't official yet. But like I said, you've been loyal to us, and I want to prove to you that we're loyal in return." Vale looked up at him, pushing forward into Hoyt's personal space, a tight smile on his face that turned Hoyt's stomach.

Was this the same smile he'd given Wallace when he'd

offered him a deal? Hoyt could picture such a smile on the snake in the Garden of Eden as he offered a tasty apple to eat.

"The board has met, and we've decided. Rebecca West won't be sheriff here for much longer."

Hoyt frowned. That was not at all what he'd been expecting to hear. "What do you mean?"

His smile became even tighter. "I mean, we're going to oppose her election in November."

"That…" He considered his words carefully, but he'd never been good at playing politics or playing nice. "That sounds like a terrible plan. Don't you need a solid reason to do something like that?"

Vale laughed, looking around the empty lobby. "I think the last two months have given us plenty of reasons to challenge her. Look at what she's done to our once-peaceful town."

"What she's done?" Hoyt refused to let this tiny reptile of a man pin him against the door, and he stepped around him to set his things down on Viviane's desk. Then he turned to face Vale with his arms crossed. "You mean solving all those weird crimes that started before she even got here? The one she volunteered to help us solve?"

The smile finally melted off Vale's face, showing his snarl. "Crime has increased a hundredfold. We've got bodies washing up on our beaches. Children are going missing. Now there's drug dealers too?"

Hoyt shook his head. "We had all those before Rebecca showed up. Don't you remember? Drug dealers being picked up and hauled off every weekend. Kids going missing. Sometimes it was their bodies washed up on the shore too."

"I understand that, but—"

"The ocean is a big place with strong currents." Hoyt was going to say what he needed to say without interruption from this man. "None of these recent ones are even local. The only reason we're involved in the cases is because of the wind and the currents. Nothing to do with Rebecca being sheriff."

Vale raised a finger. "I—"

"And may I remind you that she's solved those cases? So the crime rate is clearly not on her." Hoyt raised a finger too. "On the other hand, our—"

"Our numbers are still going up," Vale blustered, saliva peppering his lips. "Soon, we'll have crime rates as bad as our neighbors. And you and I both know that's not how we do things on Shadow Island."

Hoyt snorted. "It's not how it used to be done, true."

Vale's nostrils flared. "Rebecca can't follow our protocol. She doesn't fit in. I was willing to give her a shot, thinking she could learn. Or that someone would teach her. But it's clear now that she'll never be the kind of sheriff we need here."

"You want a sheriff who doesn't solve the crimes we've always had?"

"I want a sheriff who doesn't rock the boat!" Vale wiped spittle from his lips. "We're on an island. Anyone who rocks the boat here needs to be removed. And that needs to happen before we all sink."

Hoyt leaned forward, peering down at the scaly little prick. "If you'd spent any time on the water or hanging out with any fishermen, you'd know that sometimes you've got to rock the boat. Especially when there's a snake hiding under the seats, waiting to strike."

"Why are you arguing with me?" Vale raged, slashing his arms outward. "You can only benefit moving forward. There'd be an open position left. One you could take. A sheriff makes more than a deputy, you know. And I could find ways for you to make even more money than from just your salary."

There it was. The line he'd been waiting for. And no way to record it.

"I'd be making as much as Wallace was?" Hoyt said it as if he knew how much money his friend had been making.

Vale smiled. "At least as much."

"Look how much good that did him." Hoyt pointed to the memorial plaque on the wall. "You care so much for him, but you never even came by to pay your respects. Then again, I guess you thought you'd paid him enough already. Right?"

Vale's eyes narrowed, and his lip curled. "Just remember which side you should be on, Frost. There's only one winning side. You could make this a good thing for everyone, or you could make things harder on yourself. You don't want to end up on the wrong side." His gaze drifted to the memorial picture. "You don't want to end up like your predecessors."

Before the last syllable had left his lips, Vale turned and stormed out of the building.

Frost looked, staring at the security camera that covered the entire lobby. He needed to check those and see if they'd been tampered with. It shouldn't be possible, since the terminal was locked up in the sheriff's office—another place Vale shouldn't have a key to. Only Rebecca should have that key.

Before he did that, though, he needed to get a locksmith out here to change the locks, all the locks, from the front door to the evidence locker, so nothing like this could ever happen again.

24

The waiting area of Senator Overbay's office in the Hart Senate Office Building could've been mistaken for a therapist's office if one ignored the Virginia state seals plastered on everything. Plaques, business cards, framed artwork, even the back of the secretary's leather chair was embossed with it.

At least the chairs were comfortable. Rebecca expected she'd be kept waiting for at least an hour. Longer if the senator was petty. The original appointment time was for eight but had been pushed to eleven. That was a common tactic people in power used to let others know just how important they were.

And how unimportant I am.

Maybe if she was lucky, she could even get a power nap in.

"Sheriff West?"

Rebecca stopped getting comfortable in the chair to look at the secretary. He was a fun mix between sleek professional and lean boxer. Or maybe he did MMA. Either way, though he seemed to handle his duties well, he walked and held himself like a man more used to physical work. Maybe he was a recently retired Marine.

"Yes?"

There were plenty of Marines and Air Force officers walking around these office buildings. As well as white-haired men in ten-thousand-dollar suits and women in thousand-dollar heels with complicated updos. Rebecca had taken the time to change into a pantsuit and freshen up before coming here, but she didn't come close to fitting in with her off-the-rack clothing.

"Ma'am?" He was now staring at her with lifted eyebrows and standing beside his desk.

"Hmm?"

"You can go in now, ma'am."

She checked the clock, saw it was eleven on the dot, and was surprised at the punctuality. "Oh. Sorry, it's been a long morning."

"Yes, ma'am. Traveling can be a beast."

Uncrossing her legs, she stood.

He opened the thick oak door that led to the senator's private office and waved her through.

"Thank you."

"Ah, Sheriff West, thank you for coming up. And I'm sorry about the delay." The senator stood, holding his tie with one hand as he leaned over his desk to shake her hand.

While she knew from the news, and from the file she'd read, that Paul Overbay was only in his early sixties, his deep chestnut hair was almost completely replaced by gray with streaks of white.

"No apologies needed, Senator. I'm sure you have more pressing matters." Keeping the sneer out of her voice was easy. She'd been dealing with politicians and criminals long enough to be used to it.

"FEMA waits for no man, Sheriff." Senator Overbay rubbed his hand over his tired eyes.

That was not the response she'd expected. "FEMA?"

"I've been trying to get disaster housing updated all week-end. I have to stay on the ball to make sure it all goes through. Flooding has lasting effects on homes, and some of the people who were back in theirs can no longer stay there. I'm sure you know all about that. Your county was one of the ones hit by Hurricane Boris."

"Yes, sir, we were hit pretty hard. Thankfully, the flooding was kept at bay. Our storm surge ebbed almost as quickly as it flowed."

"Due to your hard work, so I've heard. Everyone I spoke with said you and your men worked with the citizens to build sandbag barriers while evacuating the residents. Well done."

Rebecca was not comfortable with so many compliments, so she deflected. "My staff and I, along with many residents. We're a small town, sir. We all work together when times get tough. And I relied heavily on those more experienced in such matters to tell me what to do."

"Clearly they knew what they were doing. I've had my people checking in periodically with all the counties that were hit, making sure they have what they need for recov-ery. Your Mayor Doughtie spoke very highly of you. Please, sit."

He motioned to the leather couch and matching wood-framed accent chairs on the other side of the small, round antique coffee table in the center of a navy-blue rug. It made a nice little sitting area separate from his desk. He crossed his hands in front of his body, waiting. It was clear he had no plan to sit until she did.

Rebecca sat down in one of the accent chairs. So far, the senator hadn't been anything like she'd expected. "And I would like to extend my condolences on the loss of your son."

Overbay twitched as if he'd been struck by a leg cramp while trying to sit.

Rebecca winced at her poor timing.

"Thank you, Sheriff." He sat down in the other chair, taking the time to clear his throat and smooth his suit coat. Not because he was vain, but to have enough time to gather himself. Rebecca noted the sheen of tears in his eyes.

"Would you like to tell me about him?" This time, her voice was soft. "Talking about loved ones is the best way to keep them alive, at least for a few more hours."

"He was my oldest child. My only son." He cleared his throat, paying entirely too much attention to straightening the line of his trousers that clung to his too-thin legs. The senator didn't just look older than his age, he looked stretched thin and worn. "He was a grown man. Lived on his own. But, still, he was my child. Parents don't…they never stop being parents. Do you know what I mean?" His eyes begged for her understanding.

"I understand the concept. I know my own parents were always there for me. Cheering me on every step of the way. But I don't have any children myself."

"They're a blessing and a curse." Overbay bit his lip and shook his head. "It is a blessing. It is. However, when your children start doing things you know will hurt them, it becomes difficult."

That was the perfect lead-in for Rebecca. "What did your son start doing?"

Overbay bit his lip again. He glanced over at the door, then up at the clock. "Things that could be used in an attempt to blackmail me."

His unwillingness to answer her question was a bit surprising. She'd just started to think he was serious about this meeting and actually wanted to be open and honest so they could get things settled. Instead, he was already deflecting. "Sir, why did you ask me up here if you aren't willing to answer questions?"

"I've heard you'll do whatever it takes to uphold the law. That's what I need now." Overbay nodded at the door. "Gunny tells me you're someone to be trusted."

"Gunny?"

"I'm sorry. My secretary, Gunnery Sergeant Kline. Retired." Casually, he pointed toward the door. "When your name came up in connection with my son's case, he thought I should trust you. He said he'd heard about you. I believe you're the best person to handle this situation." His face showed no emotions at all. He'd finally managed to rein in his grief.

"And why don't you trust the VSP?"

"I don't distrust the state police, Sheriff. I simply trust you more. I know you don't care about my office, my," he snorted, "political power, my money, or who you have to take down to get justice. That's who I need to find out who killed my son."

That was so direct and emotional that Rebecca didn't doubt it for a second. Which was surprising. Overbay might've been one of the few honest politicians. "I believe you. So why don't you tell me about—"

"I prefer not to discuss my family drama in a work setting." He waved his hand around his office. "How do you feel about grabbing an early lunch?"

25

The senator chose to have lunch at Charlie Palmer. No shock there. It was a well-known restaurant for working lunches and had just opened for the day when they walked in. Overbay had a word with the maître d' and silently passed him a wad of folded bills.

Rebecca couldn't see how much it was, but there must've been several, considering how thick the wad was.

They were escorted past the floating cubes of wine bottles in the center of the restaurant to the private rooms in the back.

Gunnery Sergeant Kline stopped before the door to the room and sat down at a table by himself. It was completely out of place right next to the door. He was sitting there like a guard, protecting the senator's privacy. This explained why Overbay'd handed so much money over at the start. He'd rented out this private room to have this conversation.

A single table was set up, and a waiter was on hand to take their orders immediately—Senator Overbay was either in a hurry or wanted privacy. Rebecca was betting on the latter. No one wanted to share family drama, as he had called it, with the waitstaff. He gave his order for drink and food as he sat down. The server pulled her chair, then presented the menu.

It wasn't on her dime, and she'd been forced to make a last-minute flight at this man's request, but Rebecca still couldn't stomach the idea of sticking taxpayers with those inflated lunch-menu prices. "Grilled chicken club."

The server nodded, then ducked out. There and gone without a word.

"Thank you for waiting. I know this must seem like such a waste of time." Overbay meticulously shifted his silverware around on the table.

As true as that might be, Rebecca was too polite to say so out loud.

"I'm just not comfortable talking about my family or personal life while at work. Too many ways things could go wrong. With your line of work, I'm sure you understand. And when you…well, when I finish explaining…" He paused for a breath. "I'm sorry. I'm…I admit I'm a bit off my game. If people found out, I would be swarmed by sharks faster than you could blink." He smiled, trying to make it seem like a joke, but his eyes were too watery for humor.

And just like that, Rebecca remembered this was a grieving father. With him surrounded by luxury and the pomp of politics on the drive over in the limo and aides darting around him like a school of fish, it was too easy to forget that fact. He'd heard about his son's death less than twenty-four hours earlier. He seemed like he was doing the best he could to keep working while he struggled.

Raw memories of the murder of her parents flooded Rebecca's thoughts. Her heart clenched, and she had to consciously harden her features. Only five years ago, she'd lost them both in the blink of an eye. And that had been at the behest of a different senator, one not nearly as noble as the man across the table from her now. To show him the same compassion she'd been shown, she cut him a bit more slack.

"I remember how difficult it was to hold myself together after I lost my parents. You've barely had time to even start grieving."

"You understand. We're public servants. The job may not always come first, but it must get done regardless." He nodded. "My wife is at home, trying to plan a funeral. I haven't found the strength yet to tell her it'll have to be a closed casket."

His voice started to whine as he struggled to hold in a sob. He had to stop and clear his throat twice, dabbing his eyes with the linen napkin.

"I'm so sorry, Senator." And she was.

He waved a hand. "But we're off the clock now. Ask me any questions you wish. I want to catch these people."

That was something Rebecca completely understood. "Which people?"

"Let me start at the beginning. I'm sorry I had to play cloak-and-dagger with you, but you'll understand why. Nearly a month ago, I received a text message on my private phone. It was a blackmail threat with a video attached to it."

"And what was the video of?"

Overbay pulled a phone out of his interior breast pocket —not the BlackBerry she'd seen him using to respond to emails before but a different one. He started tapping on the screen. "Keep in mind, this is my private phone. This number isn't public knowledge. As I'm sure you've been told, I've already turned this matter over to the FBI. And as far as I know, they haven't been able to track down who sent it."

He set the phone on the table and slid it over to Rebecca, looking away.

Intrigued, she picked it up. The blackmail letter was fairly basic and just as Benji had described. She clicked on the video attached to the message.

"It's a bit, um...*risqué* doesn't do it justice." Overbay dropped his head, covering his face with one hand.

Rebecca found the volume button and muted the video. He'd already watched it once, presumably. He didn't need to hear it again now.

It was evident within the first moment what was happening. Frederick Overbay snorted cocaine out of the belly button of a barely dressed, strung-out woman stretched across the lap of another woman who appeared to be naked. As Frederick finished his bump, he leaned back, facing the camera. He was also wearing next to nothing, just a thin robe that wasn't properly tied and showed more of his body than she'd seen when he was pulled out of the ocean.

A drug-fueled orgy—she peered closely—in what could be a luxury hotel of some kind. She was certain Benji and whoever else was working on this would nail down the date, time, and precise location soon enough.

Another woman in the background—barely legal, if at all —fell out of the lap of the man she'd been making out with. Chester Able. He was flushed and also only wearing a robe that wasn't tied at all.

Rebecca tapped the screen and saw that she was only two minutes into a forty-minute video.

"I'm going to need a copy of this."

"Of course. I can send you a copy or the FBI can. However you want."

She'd learned during her years with the Bureau that certain apps allowed for high-speed transmission of video messages. Nonetheless, she was surprised the senator had such an app on his personal phone.

Tapping the screen, she jumped along in the video, looking for anyone else she might recognize. There was a light knock at their door, and Rebecca paused the video and dropped the phone in her lap, where she covered it with her napkin.

The senator smiled at her caution. "Gunny, come on in." Overbay waved his hand, motioning the man over.

"Your lunches, sir."

Rebecca twisted to look over her shoulder at the door. Gunny, not a member of the staff, was holding a tray. He closed the door firmly behind him before walking over with their dishes. None of them spoke as the tray was set down. Overbay indicated her plate, and they were both served. His job done, Gunny turned and left them alone again.

"Did you pay what they demanded?"

Overbay nodded as he pushed around the pasta on his plate. "I had to. If that video got out, it would hurt my reputation, but it would destroy his life. I'm old. I can retire at any time. But my son is young still. He has his whole life—" He realized what he'd been about to say, and his eyes flinched with the shock of pain.

Without thinking, Rebecca reached over and placed her hand on his. The skin was loose and thin, covering barely more than bones. This was not the same man she'd watched argue on the senate floor just a few months ago while both sides fought about the budget.

This man was broken, barely holding on while he tried to wrap his mind around what had happened to his family.

"He had his whole life ahead of him. The drugs, this, was all new. My son was a good man. I don't know what went so wrong for him recently that he felt he had to turn to drugs to deal. But the man in that video, that's not the son I raised and was so proud of. He had a life, a career, and a loving fiancée. I wanted to protect that."

"Did you ask him about it?"

Overbay donned a paternal smile followed by a pat on her

hand as he gestured to her food. "I did. He refused to talk about it. He claimed it was just a party that got out of hand, that he didn't have a problem. I also reached out to his fiancée to see if she knew about the drugs. I couldn't bring myself to tell her about the other women. She told me he was a grown man and knew what he was doing. I never did like her much."

Rebecca took a bite of her sandwich, then pointed her fork at his plate, encouraging him to eat as well. She knew food was probably the last thing on his mind, but he'd clearly skipped too many meals recently.

"Did you recognize anyone else in the videos?" She pondered how the restaurant had managed to make a glorified BLT with chicken taste so good.

On second thought, for twenty-four bucks, it better be.

He shook his head, taking a tiny bite of his food. "No one. And I watched the whole thing three times. It's not like I could show the video to other people to find out if they recognized anyone either. My wife would have a heart attack if she saw what her son was doing."

While he might not know how to take screenshots and remove the background, Rebecca certainly did. And she would be doing that and sharing them until she had names for every person in the video.

"Sheriff, I want to make myself very clear here." Overbay paused until Rebecca looked him in the eyes. "I want my son's killers found. I want the people responsible for that video prosecuted. I do not want that video to get leaked to the press."

He paused, and she started to bristle as she waited for him to try and order her around.

"Sir. I—"

He held up a hand. "If it does get leaked, and it most likely will, since I will not be paying any more hush money, I would like a warning, if possible. That way, I have time to alert my remaining family. I'm praying I don't have to do that until after we lay him to rest. His mother shouldn't have that thrown in her face without notice."

Once again, Rebecca was surprised by this man. He was a career politician, yet he still seemed focused on his family and hadn't said a single thing about losing his reelection. That was something all politicians worried about in her experience. Having the job was more important than actually doing the job.

She studied his frail form, his watery eyes, and wondered if he was really the grieving, devoted father, husband, and public servant he was pretending to be. Or was he just a really good actor who was playing her for his own political gain?

26

Darian wiped a dab of mayo from the side of his mouth. "Is there anything better than a fresh chicken-salad sandwich on a hot summer day?"

The office was refreshingly quiet, with Hoyt out assisting the state police as they continued their search for the shooter. It was his way of getting out of computer work. Most outside security devices had been destroyed in the hurricane and very few had been replaced so far. Still, there was video footage to comb through from the remaining security cameras they'd found in the area.

"A strawberry milkshake to go with it." Viviane nodded as she played with her straw, causing it to squeak as it slid through the plastic lid.

"Strawberry and tomato!" Darian gulped down his food and shook his head in disgust. "That sounds awful. No, thank you. I'll stick with my water."

"Water and wheat bread!" Viviane mimicked him. "That's awful. No, thanks."

He opened his mouth to retort but she reached up and tapped her earpiece to answer a call on her headset. "Shadow

Island Sheriff's Department, how may I help you?" She spun back to her desk to take notes.

Darian tuned her out and went back to searching for connections between Frederick Overbay and Chester Able. It should've been quick work, since Overbay didn't have any kind of criminal record. However, given his father was an influential member of Congress, Darian didn't trust that fact. Instead, he was checking previous residences and reaching out to those police departments to ask if there was anything he should know that hadn't made it into any official reports.

So far, he'd come up with nothing more than two moving violations and another one that was written off as a verbal warning. Either the senator's son wasn't a dirtbag, or he was an expert at hiding it.

"Hudson? I'm transferring a call to you." He looked up as Viviane was walking over, a note in hand. "Lettinger says she's got a match for the third body. We're basically a joint task force on this thing now, right?"

"No clue."

She shrugged and turned back to her desk, looking reluctant to do so.

Darian rolled his eyes, disappointed she'd retreated so quickly. "Hey, you're the one who wants to learn more about the case and how to be a cop."

She spun around, her eyes sparking with interest. "I sure am."

He motioned for her to return. "Why would a VSP special agent need to inform me about the identity of a murder victim in this case?"

"Um..." Viviane dropped into the seat of the spare desk with the new, fully functional computer setup. "Well, obviously it's because it's linked to our case with Chester Able."

"That's an assumption." Darian stuffed the rest of his

sandwich into his mouth, talking around it. "What's the reason?"

"Oh! Because they have the same M.O."

He waved for her to continue as he plugged the name on Viviane's note into the system and cross-referenced it with Able and Overbay. When she shook her head, he continued his prompting. "That's a better reason. Do you know how we figure out the real reason?"

Viviane furrowed her eyebrows as she thought about it. "I don't."

"Neither do I. That's why we answer this call and ask her." He chuckled at her sudden ire.

"That's what I told you to do!"

"Yup, so let's find out the reason now that we have our theories. Police work is a lot like the scientific method. Look at what you have, make a theory, then test the theory. Remember that." He hit speakerphone before letting his finger hover over the blinking call button. "That's what West pushes, and it's served her well. That way, if things don't turn out the way we theorized, it shows us that we were missing information before we made our theory."

"Which helps us figure out what information we were missing." Viviane nodded and rolled her chair next to his desk.

"Yup. Think like that, and it'll help you figure out cases, and not just the annoying questions I ask you during training."

Viviane lightly punched his arm. "I do appreciate the lessons, even if you make them annoying."

He snorted. "That's another lesson for you. Most police work is dealing with annoying people, places, and things." He wrinkled his nose. "And smells. Now, let's not keep her on hold any longer."

"Lettinger, it's Hudson. Viviane said you wanted to tell me about the identification you made?"

"Yes, I've got Frost out here with me, but he said you're the one who's digging into possible links between the victims."

"I am, but right now, I'm focused on Overbay." Darian reread the name on the note. "I haven't heard of this guy, Landon Hannity. Do you want me to check if he's linked with the senator's kid? I can look for him specifically if you need me to dig into it more while you're out there, if you know where he's from."

There was a long pause. "Um, Deputy Hudson, Hannity is one of yours."

Viviane cocked her head like a confused puppy. "One of ours? Did you arrest him once?"

Darian opened a search for their local database of records. He didn't remember the name, but then, there were a lot of tourists who came through too.

"He lives on Shadow Island. He's one of your locals. That's what I'm saying. Do you not have a missing persons file on him already? It's been three days, at least."

Viviane shook her head when Darian frowned at her. "Landon? I don't even *know* anyone by that name."

"Me either." Viviane and her family knew almost everyone on the island. If she hadn't met them, Darian would've bet they were most likely introverted or flew under the radar intentionally. Both were possible in this instance, especially if Hannity was a drug dealer.

"Who's with you?" Rhonda sounded annoyed.

"You don't recognize our dispatcher and current gumshoe, Viviane Darby?" Hudson guffawed.

"Viviane? Yes. Sorry. You sound different."

"I'm using my best soon-to-be sleuth voice, Rhonda. That's why."

Darian was not in the least bit surprised that the two women were already on a first name basis.

"Oh, that makes sense. Anyway, I'm guessing you don't have a missing persons report to go with this?"

Neither of them even needed to look that up. "We haven't had a missing person since mid-June, when Sylvie Harper was kidnapped." Darian found the name on the DMV site. "Yeah, he's one of ours. He's got a place at the apartments over on Beachview."

"Okay, well, since he's a local, do you think you could pull up everything you have on him and get back to me?"

"Will do. I can tell you now, though, he doesn't have a record with us."

"Which makes sense if he's been working off the island." Rhonda let out a frustrated sigh. "That's two guys who don't have a drug record and only one who does. This may not be as drug related as we thought. Or maybe the other two were innocent bystanders in this deal and Chester was the target. It makes sense, since Chester was nearly killed in his hospital bed too. You don't sneak into a hospital with a syringe full of potassium unless you have a lot of balls, a lot of experience, or both."

"Especially with the sheriff's cruiser parked right out front." Viviane leaned forward so she could be heard better. "They were willing to risk it even knowing she was inside."

"Found him." Darian tapped the screen, calling Viviane's attention to it. He'd switched from searching police records to social media instead. "He worked as a deckhand on a charter fishing boat out of Coastal Ridge."

"That explains why his boss didn't report him as missing. Those jobs are seasonal, with people coming and going all the time. We'll have to talk to Shen, the landowner, to see how long he'd been living here. He could be a new import."

Viviane tapped his screen, and Darian clicked the link she wanted.

"He's got a recent post, talking about how he's opening his own business. Says, 'Hannity Charters will be opening soon.' His post goes on to say that he's getting the last of the money he needs for his startup funds and to keep an eye out for more updates and pictures of his new boat. That was three days ago." Darian checked the time on the post. "He posted that the morning before he died."

Lunch was over. They had a new lead to follow.

27

S eated as she was in a small conference room, the quiet lull of industrial air-conditioning had never tweaked Rebecca's nerves as much as it did now. Back in the days when she fit in at the FBI, it'd been soothing background noise, helping her focus.

No longer was that the case.

She'd been escorted to the confining space by Benji. Without her former credentials, she wasn't permitted to walk about freely. An agent from Cyber had arrived shortly afterward with a flash drive and adaptor, then insisted on inspecting her official Shadow Island sheriff's tablet to check for security problems before allowing her access to the blackmail video. He also insisted that she sign transfer paperwork, which she'd been more than happy to do.

Not one to let a good resource go to waste, she handed him her personal and professional phones and asked him to check those over as well. While he did that, Rebecca started the data transfer, then waited until the agent was done with his checks. He was only an agent, and even Benji hadn't seen what was in this file yet. Just because he had the thumb drive didn't mean he was on the case or allowed to see what was on it.

They exchanged devices, and he finally left her in the empty room to go through this newest piece of evidence. Pulling out a notepad and pen, she mentally prepared herself for what she would be watching. Then clicked play.

The little section she'd seen earlier was nothing compared to the beginning. The video opened with the senator's son having sex with one of the women, bending her over a couch, taking dirty talk to a whole new level. It was hard to imagine he wasn't paying for the woman's services. She'd find that out soon enough as, later, every word would have to be transcribed and documented.

For now, she tuned him out and focused on the other people in the frame. She also noted that the camera, which she imagined was someone's phone, was being carried around before it was set on a table for a broader view of the lavish hotel suite.

Deep in the background, Chester Able walked into view and sat in the chair she'd seen him in before. Rebecca noted down the time stamp of his appearance. Another woman walked into frame behind him, and he nodded ever so slightly at her, in a way that felt conspiratorial to Rebecca. They talked for a bit before getting physical.

Overbay finished with his partner, who stretched out across the couch she'd been bent over. Meanwhile, he walked over and briefly spoke with Able before disappearing from view.

With them farther away from the camera, it was hard to hear what they were saying. When Overbay returned a minute later, he had a little baggie in one hand and a scantily clad woman holding the other. Three young women were now on screen. One stretched out on top of the first woman, and they started making out for a bit before

Overbay joined them and repositioned the second woman on her back.

The video was back to the scene she'd already watched. He sprinkled the cocaine into her belly button and snorted it out. Able either finished or fizzled out, then everyone sat down and had a few drinks as they recovered from their activities. That was when the screen went blank, and Rebecca looked at the time stamp, ready to note that too. Except the time kept ticking and there were several minutes left on the recording. The phone must've fallen over.

Rebecca cranked the volume higher until she could hear a conversation going on in the background. It wasn't about anything useful. They talked about what drinks and how much coke they had left. From the context, they were on at least day two of this bender.

There were a few clunks, then the video came back. The prostitute—they sure seemed like hired workers by this point —Overbay had been with at the beginning was leaning over the couch. Again. She set the phone back up, discreetly, watching to make sure no one else could see what was happening. The woman might not have been the person who'd started the recording earlier, but she was in on the subterfuge at the very least.

Rebecca noted an appendage—an elbow—just barely on the screen to one side. It was bare but unmoving. She couldn't even tell if it belonged to a man or a woman. Adding this to her notes, she also noted the time stamp. Could he be the third victim they found? Or even the killer?

The door to the suite opened, and an older man strode in. His neck was tight, and his face turned red with anger as he glared around the room. Older Dude looked familiar, but Rebecca couldn't quite place him, with his face so far away from the camera and twisted in rage.

Older Dude started yelling, and they all jumped. All the

women got up and huddled together, inching their way off-screen. Older Dude continued yelling but at someone else outside of view. Maybe at Elbow Person, given the direction of his ranting. She couldn't tell if anyone was responding, but Able and Overbay watched, pulling their robes closed tight.

Rebecca paused the video and grabbed a screenshot before starting again. Older Dude, who was yelling at Able and Overbay now, eventually stopped screaming and stormed out the door.

The party boys convened, clearly discussing the intruder as they kept pointing at the door while arguing. Two of the women cautiously walked back into view and joined the conversation.

Then the off-camera woman must've picked up the phone and stopped the recording.

Rebecca rewound the video, frame by frame, until she found a good angle to study Older Dude. She took a second screenshot, then cropped both shots and emailed them to Hoyt. Older Dude was so familiar to her. He was someone she'd seen, and recently. That meant he had to be from Shadow Island.

That was enough for now. Rebecca checked the time. It was just before two. Which left her plenty of wiggle room to visit one more place before she left for home.

28

R ebecca swallowed hard, forcing all emotion from her face.

"You're sure about this?" Benji took his glasses off and peered past Rebecca out the passenger-side window.

She turned away from the sobering view of every possible style of grave marker outside the car and looked him in the eye. He was in the driver's seat, wrist propped on the steering wheel, a questioning look on his face. Down deep, where he kept it hidden from most people, Rebecca knew Benji was a kind man. And he was just worried about her.

"I'll be fine. I can handle this." Before she lost her nerve, she grabbed her bag, pulling the strap over her shoulder. "Once I'm done here, I'll call a taxi to take me to the airport. You can't keep using me as an excuse to play hooky anymore."

He rolled his eyes and shook his head. "That's not what this is about. I mean, yeah, getting out of work is nice, but are you sure you're up for this? You've been going nonstop all day. You must be tired. Let me drive you to a hotel so you can get some rest and you can tackle this tomorrow."

As if she could ever sleep easily in this town again. "I appreciate your concern. I really do. But I can handle this. I need to do this. And I'll sleep better in my own bed tonight." Rebecca opened the door to hop out but paused when he touched her arm.

"Take care of yourself, Rebecca. It was good to see you again."

She smiled, but he'd already put his glasses back on, hiding behind his reflective lenses, and he turned back toward the road ahead. "You, too, Benji." She climbed out of the car and shut the door.

As her feet hit the thick grass of the lawn, the black sedan pulled away, leaving her alone. Alone with pain clutching her stomach and twisting it in knots. Her thoughts immediately started racing, going through everything she had to say, everything she should do. Everything she'd failed to do before.

Rebecca counted the grave markers, looking for the right row. This was the first time she'd been here since the funeral. She'd even had to look up the location on the plot map to figure out where to go.

It was a bittersweet walk. While the grounds were gorgeous—an ocean of emerald green dotted with a geometric pattern of gray marble slabs and statues—the reality of who she was visiting made each step heavier. She reached the correct row and turned to walk down the line, reading each name as she went.

Then she reached the marker she was looking for.

Rebecca pulled the strap of her bag off her shoulder. Although there were barely any clouds in the midday sky, gloom and longing squeezed her heart. Sitting down in the grass, she pulled her bag onto her lap, hugging it tightly as she stared at the glossed marble.

"Hi, Mom, Dad. I'm sorry it took so long to come see

you." She stared at the names Bruce and Anna West on the shared headstone. A tear streaked down her cheek, and she made no effort to brush it away, knowing others would soon follow. "I…moved away. I had to. But I did find the men who were responsible. Not just the man who…"

Blood on the sheets.

Blood on the cupboards.

Mom's dead eyes staring.

A sob ripped free from Rebecca's throat, and she clutched her bag tightly. "So much has changed since I lost you. I quit the FBI. I know you were proud of me getting that job, but it wasn't what I needed anymore. I'm trying to move on, but I miss you both so much." Rebecca let the tears flow, watering the grass in front of her parents' grave.

After several minutes, her grief eased, and she straightened her back. The events of her life played like a vintage movie reel in her mind. Her dead parents were an image she knew she'd never shake. But she'd hoped those images would be replaced with the good memories from Shadow Island. Holding onto the pain of the past felt like an anchor around her neck. She needed to come to terms with the events that had shaped her life.

"I haven't really trusted people since I lost you. Calvin and I broke up because of those trust issues. When you feel like even the government can't be trusted…or people in power…well, losing the two people I loved more than anything shook me to my core. But I'm trying. I know my skepticism about people's motives builds walls between me and others. It's an exhausting battle between past wounds and…"

She realized she could vaguely see her own reflection in the headstone. A tiny smile pulled up the corners of her mouth, which she'd been told all her life she got from her mom.

"Let me start at the beginning. I was only supposed to be taking an extended vacation on Shadow Island. The same place we always stayed. Do you remember Ryker Sawyer? That local boy I played with…"

29

"Deputy Hudson, quit your slacking!" Hoyt slipped through the half door at the station. Rebecca's fob was on the keys hanging from his pocket and let him through without needing Viviane to buzz him in, a fact he took advantage of whenever he could. It was the only upside of standing in for the sheriff.

"Senior Deputy Frost, quit talking out your ass!" Darian didn't even bother looking up from his computer, but he did give his fellow deputy the one-finger salute.

Hoyt guffawed. Okay, one other upside of being the stand-in was getting to bust Darian's balls and not worry about their boss catching him. "If I did that, I'd never talk to you." He waited 'til Darian started smirking. "After all, the only language you speak is shit-talk."

Viviane was standing at the kitchenette table, giggling to herself.

"It's the only language I use with you." Darian pointed his pen at Hoyt as he dropped down in his seat. "That's all you deserve." He flipped the pen around and, without looking, pointed it at Viviane. "I chat with her all the time. We talk about highbrow things you wouldn't understand."

Hoyt turned his nose up and lifted his pinky from his coffee mug as he took a loud slurp, making Viviane giggle again and roll her eyes. "Well, I do declare. Highbrow conversations, you say. Does that mean you've finished digging into Landon Hannity and figured out how he fits into our case here?"

"Hannity stated he just bought a new boat, but we haven't found it. He supposedly got it Thursday or maybe Friday morning. Registration might not have been filed yet, or it was but hasn't gone through. There was a post he made about pictures he planned to share, but we haven't found any of them either. So we don't know any details. A charter boat, clearly, but no make or model."

"And of course, you haven't gone by his apartment to look around." Hoyt sighed and *tsk*ed at them both. "Good thing you have your senior deputy here to save your asses."

Before he could continue giving them grief over nothing, Viviane scoffed. "I already talked to Shen. That's the landowner, in case you didn't know, Senior Deputy Frost. I let him know that the state police would be there shortly to go through Hannity's place. I also found out that he did work on a charter fishing boat, but he never put in enough hours to even make rent. Which means he was getting his money from elsewhere and most likely using his job for tax purposes only." She looked down her nose at him snootily.

Hoyt clutched his hand to his chest. "*Et tu*, Viviane?"

"Don't start none, won't be none." She shook her finger in Hoyt's face as she strode past him, regal as a queen, and perched on her throne at the dispatch desk.

"Yeah, she's ready." Hoyt turned away from Viviane and shared an approving nod with Darian. "Our little girl is all grown up."

"She can certainly hold her own now. Hard to believe she used to run around playing cops and robbers with her little pigtails bobbing and—"

"I never wore pigtails."

"Anyway," Hoyt waved them both off, "I knew where Hannity lived. He's been there since he moved back around seven years ago."

"Wait." Darian frowned hard enough that his downturned mouth furrowed his five o'clock shadow. "You knew Hannity?"

"Not like a friend, but yeah. I picked him up for drunk driving. Wallace took care of him 'til he was sober and..." And there it was. The connection. "Wallace took over the paperwork too."

"Which explains why we didn't find anything on him. Wallace would've kept those records on paper only." Darian gave him another one-finger salute. "Not my fault I didn't find anything."

"But that means all we have to do is find his paperwork in the stack Wallace left us." Viviane slapped her palms on her thighs and hopped down from her chair. "Where are they? I'll help dig through them."

Hoyt's stomach twisted, and all his focus was on the keys in his pocket. "Let's let West handle that when she gets back. I don't want to mess up the order, if she even thinks there's some kind of order. I might have screwed it up once already and don't want to make things worse."

That was only partially true. The whole truth was, he didn't want either of them touching the files. If things went down the way Rebecca had said Wallace planned, he didn't want them to be attached to it in any way. He realized he now viewed those files as tainted. They were just one more symptom of the cancer that'd been allowed to grow in his town.

Viviane was just starting her career. Hudson was settling into his with a new family to protect. Hoyt...felt a surge of empathy for Alden. This had to be what he was feeling when he'd been given the choice years ago. He could protect his people, knowing he didn't have much to lose and they had everything ahead of them. Or he could drag good people down with him.

In the privacy of his own thoughts, Hoyt knew he'd likely have done the same back then as well. He didn't have Rebecca's determination, iron will, or expertise when dealing with such tricky situations.

"Frost? You okay there? You look like you've seen a ghost."

Hoyt sighed and looked over at Darian, who was staring at him.

"Yeah, I'm fine. I just remembered how much paperwork I have to fill out now and really wish the boss was back already." Knowing how easily he could have turned to the dark side left a huge weight in his belly.

30

The hum of airplane engines fighting gravity mixed with departure and arrival announcements made it hard for Rebecca to concentrate on anything else.

"Shadow Island Sheriff's Department, this is Deputy Frost speaking."

She could barely make out her senior deputy's voice on the other end of the phone.

"Frost, it's West. Have you gotten my email yet?"

There was a long, guilty pause. "Uh, give me just a minute."

Rebecca sighed and glanced around, trying to count how many people were waiting at the gate. She'd managed to get a standby ticket at the counter. If there was a spot open on this flight, she would be back just after dark. "You forgot to check your email periodically, didn't you?"

"Uh, well, there's been a lot going on. I had to lend a hand with the search."

"Then you had to come back and give Hudson a hard time, right?" Just talking with Hoyt made Rebecca feel better. A bit of home to help ground her. Visiting her parents had been cathartic. She'd had a good cry, a long chat, and now it was time to get back to work.

"I've got the email right here." He blatantly ignored her question about Darian, which was answer enough. "Uh, Boss."

"You know him?" It was a question, but his tone let her know the answer already.

"That's Mitchell Longfellow, the treasurer of the Select Board. The one Chester Able had been calling."

A lightbulb went on in Rebecca's head as she finally put it all together. "I knew I recognized him from somewhere!"

"Yeah, that's him. Never seen him that angry before, though. Um, I've also identified a second person. Well, not a whole person, but the elbow. It belongs to Landon Hannity."

"Who's Landon Hannity?"

"He's our third victim. Lettinger and Bailey identified him this morning. Thank god boaters like to get tattoos. He had one on his arm. After enhancing the image you sent me, I sent it over to the M.E., and she confirmed it belonged to the other vic. And get this, Lettinger called us to ask about him, since she couldn't find his missing persons file."

"Missing? Wait, does that mean Hannity's a local?"

"Yes, ma'am. I've already started looking into him. He worked as a deckhand on a fishing boat and rented an apartment here for the last seven years."

"Deckhand? That explains why he didn't seem familiar. He'd be out to sea most of the time with his job." Rebecca watched the departure board as it updated.

"If he worked that often. Viviane found out he barely worked there. We don't know where he was getting his full income, but it wasn't from his day job." The pride in Hoyt's voice mirrored what she felt.

"That's my girl." Rebecca grinned, giving Hoyt a taste of his own medicine. "Well, Senior Deputy, did dispatch manage to find anything else out for you about our victim? And did any of you find any link between Able, Overbay, or Longfellow?"

"None that we could find, but then we didn't know to check Longfellow. We do know that Hannity was planning to open a new business and that he got a new boat recently."

"Which could be the boat they were on when they were shot and dumped."

"Could be, but we haven't been able to identify the boat yet."

That was annoying. They still didn't have the initial crime scene. Rhonda would be able to track that down faster than they could, however. Rebecca had to focus on what was within her power. And couch it in a way that didn't reveal the blackmail scandal the FBI was already working on. "It's a good thing I came up here, then, because I found at least one link. They've known each other for a few weeks, maybe months. They were seen partying together in D.C."

"That's strange. What would a deckhand be doing in the Capitol partying with a rich kid like Overbay?"

"The usual. Cocaine and hookers." Rebecca shrugged, even though he couldn't see it. "What about the shooter at the hospital? Were you able to identify him yet?"

"Nothing on that front. Techs took fingerprints from the doors, but they're all smudged from usage. I'm not sure we'll get anything from that. Also, that nurse, Ethan, said he'd heard a loud banging on the employee door right before it all went down."

"Did he see anyone?" As nice as it would be to get a lead, she was worried that anyone who'd seen the shooter would be in danger as well.

"No one. But it'd be easy enough to catch or stop the door from closing completely without him noticing. Then wait and follow him in."

The thought of a killer following a nurse into the hospital soured Rebecca's stomach. They needed to stop this guy already.

"Are there troopers still—"

"Plenty of troopers." He clearly knew what she was worried about and cut her off to reassure her. "Handpicked by Lettinger, even. There's two at each exterior door. Two in front of Able's room. And two more keeping an eye on things inside."

Exactly what Rebecca would've done if she'd been there. "Good. That means you're available. Go back to Longfellow's and find out why he was at a party thrown by all three of our victims with pounds of cocaine. Let him know there's video evidence of it, and make sure you record how he reacts to that. You still have the recorder, right?"

"Yeah, Boss."

An announcement came on, calling for final boarding for her flight. Rebecca picked her bags up and walked to the gate. Checking her ticket, the man at the gate nodded and waved for her to go ahead. "And Hoyt?"

"Yeah, Boss?"

The fact that Rhonda had felt it necessary to swap out so many troopers had Rebecca on edge. Was this an artifact of her lingering trust issues, or had Rhonda been proactive in removing corrupt troopers from the case?

"I'm about to get on the plane now. Watch your back until I get there."

31

Mitchell Longfellow was smiling until he saw who was standing at his door. His eyes widened and darted around, locking on Hoyt's cruiser parked on the street out front again.

It was a Monday evening, the end of rush hour, and all his neighbors were coming home, driving right past the cruiser. People would be talking all over the island before dinner was even served.

"Hey, Mitch. Thought I'd come back and give you one last chance to tell me how you know Chester Able."

The shorter man scowled viciously, nearly growling as he started to swing the door closed. "I told you, I didn't. If you have further questions—"

Hoyt put his foot in the doorway and stopped it from closing. He leaned against the doorjamb, positioning the recorder in his pocket closer. "Yeah, I already heard and wrote down your lies once. Then I got this crazy video. You want to guess who one of the stars was?"

Longfellow huffed and looked up from the boot pressed between his threshold and kickplate. "Some criminal doing something stupid and recording it, making your job even easier?"

"Close." Hoyt chuckled, speaking just a bit louder and turning his face out at the street so his voice would carry. "It was a video of you at a drug-fueled orgy with, surprise, surprise, the same drug dealer who called you so many times last week. What a coincidence. Right? The same drug dealer you claim you don't know."

Longfellow turned so pale, Hoyt thought he might end up having to call an ambulance.

"I...I..." He stumbled over the words, then started pressing the door against Hoyt's foot.

"Might want to calm down there, Mitch. Don't you know that hard-core cocaine users in your age range are more likely to have heart attacks?" He had no idea if that was true, but damn, was it nice to knock the man down a few pegs. And the more he pissed the man off, the more likely he'd incriminate himself. At least, that was his hope.

"I am not a drug user!" Longfellow hissed at Hoyt, but then suddenly stopped trying to shove the door closed. "Come inside, you fool. Why are you doing this to me? We told you, if you'd just play fair, then you could be the next sheriff."

Hoyt pulled out his phone and ignored Longfellow's demands. "Yeah, about that. It's going to be hard for you to do anything on the Select Board from prison. Does this look familiar to you?" He held up the device to show the screenshot Rebecca had sent him. He leaned forward and pointed at the screen, now resting his shoulder against the doorframe. "This is you. And this is Chester. Do you want me to show you the full video? There's more than enough hookers and blow to destroy a reputation and career in politics. Wanna see?"

Hoyt had no idea if any of that were true, but Rebecca

had messaged him on the way there on how to use this threat if Longfellow needed a push.

It was a good line, because it got Longfellow to react. He snatched at the phone, and Hoyt jerked it away. He clutched at Hoyt's arm, trying to pull him into the house. "Just come inside. My neighbors can hear you."

"Your neighbors?" Hoyt laughed, twisting out of the man's desperate grasp. "The entire state's going to hear about this. Hell, the country. One of the other men at that party, he's a senator's son. And he's dead now. You're mixed up in all this shit. Nothing's going to stop that. You're in this up to your neck."

"I didn't know. I swear, I didn't know." Longfellow shook his head convulsively.

"You didn't know what?" Hoyt put on his best angry glare, the one that made teenagers run away from the firepits they'd assembled on the beach.

It worked just as well on corrupt county treasurers too. Longfellow looked like he was about to start crying.

"No. You've got it all wrong. It's all wrong. I didn't care about anyone else in the room. I only cared about Landon. I had to get him out of there."

There had to be more to this than Longfellow showing up at a party with hookers. This felt personal.

"Why?"

"He's my son!"

Hoyt upped the intensity of his scowl, looming forward and lowering his voice. He had to be sure of what he was hearing. "Who's your son?"

"Landon. Hannity. His mother was my old housekeeper. We had a tryst before I was married, so I wasn't cheating. It was short-lived. I was stupid. She was below my status, and I let her go, of course, when she ended up pregnant."

Hoyt wanted to punch the man in the face. "Go on."

Longfellow moistened his lips. "When I got married to Brittney, a woman better suited to my needs, I had to hide Landon's existence from her. But I always paid for my son, and he knew who I was and why I had to keep things quiet." He waved at the air over his shoulder. "My wife just left for a trip to Cancún, so I can speak freely about Landon without her learning of his existence. But I'd appreciate it if you'd lower your voice so my neighbors don't hear all the scuttlebutt."

That was a lot for Hoyt to try to wrap his mind around. "Well, I need to tell you that your son is dead. Can you tell me what Chester Able had to do with your son?"

"I don't know!" The blood drained from Longfellow's face. "Wait, dead?" He was struggling to keep up.

"Yes, and sorry for your loss." The jury wouldn't be able to say that Hoyt didn't show a bit of compassion when they listened to this audio.

Longfellow began to cry, snot running from his nose, beading along his top lip. "I didn't even know that man was Chester Able until you told me just now. You never showed me a picture of him. I don't know who that man is." He sobbed and sucked the snot up into his nose with a noisy and disgusting snort. "Landon must have used his phone when calling me. I told him to switch up the phones he used to call me. He could've used that guy's phone recently."

His eyes were haunted, and he'd grown pale and seemingly frail, older than his fifty-five years. Yet Hoyt really couldn't give a rat's ass. This man hadn't given a damn about anyone at all for years. Didn't care about any of the dead or their families until now. He'd even complained about the money they might've lost with the cases they'd been working on the last few months. Hell, he hadn't even bothered to show up for Wallace's memorial or funeral.

"What does Chester have to do with my son, Frost?"

Hoyt had already told the man the connection. Perhaps grief made Longfellow unable to process the information he'd been told. But he might know more about what happened to those three men than anyone they'd spoken to so far. Only now that his own family was involved, would he be willing to talk about it?

"We pulled Landon's body out of the water yesterday. We believe he was killed the same night Chester Able was shot. Landon Hannity," he stressed the last name derisively, "was shot in the stomach and thrown into the ocean."

Hoyt was surprised Landon's biological father was affected by this gory detail. Maybe he had a tiny heart in there somewhere. "I knew he'd gotten into drugs recently. That's why I went to that party in Washington. To talk him out of it. To get him some help. I was willing to pay to send him to the best rehab center if he wanted. If he didn't, I was going to cut him off. He'd told me he no longer needed my money. He was making his own, and it was better. But he was out cold at that party, and I couldn't get through to him."

"But he still called you after that?"

Longfellow nodded, his eyes bobbing in their sockets. "He did. After he sobered up. Guess someone told him I'd been there. Or maybe he'd been more aware of me than I realized. He certainly seemed like he was out of his mind on coke that night. It was a three-day bender that he said he hardly remembered. When he called, he agreed to stop using. Said he'd only done it so no one would question him. But the money was too good to pass up, so he was going to keep dealing."

"Seems to be a lot of that going around," Hoyt drawled. While technically this was a victim's family member, he couldn't manage to dredge up any sympathy. The reference to Longfellow's own corrupt behavior flew right over the man's head. "Considering the people who killed your son have already gone after Able in the hospital, you might want to leave town. But you'll need to check in with the VSP first because I'm sure they have a whole bunch of questions for you."

"Question me?" Longfellow pulled it together enough to start paying attention again. "For what?"

"Because you were with all three victims before they were killed."

Longfellow waved that off. "I'm sure they'll understand I didn't have anything to do with this."

"Special Agent Lettinger won't understand. She will most definitely have a lot of questions for you. From the night of the party on video to the conversations you had with your biological son. And you'll need to give a DNA sample."

"DNA?" The grieving father disappeared, and the pompous ass Hoyt had always known came back with a vengeance. His eyes narrowed as he straightened, squaring his shoulders and no longer slumping. "That won't be happening. I can't get caught up in this scandal, and my wife can't know I had a son with another woman. She'd divorce me, and that would affect my career."

"That sounds like a you problem." Hoyt smirked, knowing he had everything needed to get warrants for DNA, phone records, and probably bank accounts, too, since Longfellow'd been funding Landon up until the day he died. Rebecca had been right about how useful these little recorders could be.

"Wait. Lettinger? I don't know that name. Is he one of the troopers?"

Longfellow clearly hadn't been paying enough attention. This was going to be fun if things were as they suspected. "No. *She* is not a trooper. *She* is the special agent out of Norfolk. Not one of the locals."

"Not…" He went even paler than before.

Hoyt could read Longfellow like a book now, the man

was so shaken to the core. He'd been relying on the local troopers to let him off easy. Lettinger was not a local, and definitely not a member of the good ole boys club.

And on that note, Hoyt tipped his hat and walked back to his cruiser.

32

I didn't know why the senior deputy went to Longfellow's house. I'd been sitting outside Longfellow's for a while, pondering my next steps. I had a sneaking suspicion the board member was playing both ends against the middle. and we didn't need to worry about this new player—a loose group of rich bitches who thought they could take on more organized crime.

Seeing Longfellow engage with this town, however, made me suspect he'd informed the Amados that things were under control. And watching how far he lived above his means gave me the idea Treasurer Mitchell Longfellow was also part of the rich bitch club. Which meant he was profiting from both sides. Which meant he might have the very information I needed.

And, apparently, Longfellow also had information the sheriff's department wanted.

It's bad luck to be so in the know, Mr. Longfellow.

Obviously, things weren't going well with the deputy, who refused to go inside. Then the deputy spoke loud enough for me to hear what they were saying.

"...the same drug dealer that called you so many times last week!"

"Oh, he's totally under your control," I muttered to myself as I watched Deputy Frost turn Mitchell Longfellow into a crying, shaking mess. "He'll follow orders." With idiots like Longfellow in charge of the city, it was a shock this island managed to keep the streetlights on. They couldn't do even the most basic of tasks.

After a few minutes, Longfellow managed to pull himself together. Well, at least until he saw me watching from my car. I was sure he was going to piss himself once he noticed me, so I lifted my hand and waved.

The deputy left right after, confidence and anger in every stride. When he got in his cruiser and left, my interest in Deputy Frost left with him.

As soon as the cop was around the corner, I got out of my car. It was time to get some information. Finally.

I grabbed the doorknob and twisted. It wasn't even locked. Longfellow stood in the entryway. A flash of anger crossed his face. "You've got a lot of nerve, coming here."

"I don't need nerve. I handle pansy-ass traitors like you on the daily. Must be tough being a double agent. And between a cartel and a what? A club? Do you have a secret handshake?"

Terror etched into his features, just the way I liked it.

"You keep interesting company." I jerked my chin over my shoulder. "What did he want? Didn't look like he was here ready to take on his new position."

"He came to warn me that the state police are looking into me." His eyes darted back and forth, and he tried to tuck his phone into his pocket.

"You're just making friends all over the place." I snatched the phone from his grasp. The display showed the contact information for his lawyer. "You needed your lawyer for that? I thought you had everything under control."

"I do!" He scrambled backward as I threw his phone across the room. "I was only calling my lawyer...because..." Longfellow's words stumbled to a halt. He reached out, bracing himself on the wall as he continued his slow retreat.

"Do you think your lawyer can protect you from me?"

The unmistakable smell of piss filled the foyer. But Longfellow, to his credit, didn't buckle. "Did you kill Chester Able? And...the men who were with him?"

I paused and assessed him. "They were running drugs, Mr. Longfellow. Crack is whack and all that. They were little-fish bad guys who got caught up in big-fish bad-guy business."

"Why? Why did you kill them?"

I blinked. The man was actually crying. Standing there, facing a professional killer, piss running down his pants, and he was crying real tears.

Well, if he wanted to know...

"Because they didn't give me the information I needed. But I'm sure you will."

"No. You killed my son. I'm not telling you anything."

This was an intriguing piece of information. I leaned forward.

He flinched. The scent in the air grew stronger. It was now mixed with the smell of fear, and I relished it.

"You loved your son, huh? Family is everything, isn't it? It's a shame you've lost someone so close to you, just because he wouldn't be straight with me. But you know what? If you don't tell me what I need to know, you're going to lose more of your family. I'll break both your legs, tie you to a chair, and wait for your wife to get home—"

"She's in Cancún."

"Well, that's even better. Just a phone call away. I'll break both your legs, tie you to a chair, put on a video call, and watch an army of Amado men gang-rape your wife. Unless—"

"You wouldn't."

Sick and tired of being interrupted, I darted forward. My foot caught him across the knee. A crack told me the kneecap had burst free. He screamed.

It was a good thing for me that he'd used his illegal funds to purchase such a large, private house.

Longfellow dropped to the hardwood floor, crab-walking away and stopping a few feet short of a large leather recliner. He whimpered as I stepped closer again.

"No! Wait. I can fix this!" He rolled to his side, trying to get back on his feet.

"Tell me who the suppliers are."

"I don't know that."

I lifted my foot again. He tried to scramble away, but his injured leg prevented his escape. Another *crack*, and his right knee matched his left.

After his screams of pain subsided, Longfellow managed to find his voice. "There's another run tonight. Different crew. They'll know. They'll be able to tell you. I...I didn't know Landon was involved—" His face crumpled with tears.

Finally, we were getting somewhere. I took a deep breath, stepped forward, and rested my foot on top of his right knee. Ever so slightly, I increased the pressure.

He bawled. He begged.

He talked.

After confirming the location of tonight's drop, I lifted my foot. Longfellow remained on the floor. All fight had left him. He was a broken man now. No more money would flow in, and no son would walk through the door. He'd served his purpose.

This was a residential area with neighbors, and I'd left my silencer on the boat. It was time to get creative.

And quick. I had things to do tonight.

As I picked up a heavy stone table lamp, the little bit of life left in Longfellow rose to the surface. He scrambled to get away from me.

I smashed the lamp against the side of his head. He dropped like a rock. Reaching down, I pulled the electrical cord free, yanking the plug out of the socket.

Longfellow did his best to hold on to his senses. His eyelids flickered as he rocked his head back and forth, trying to maintain consciousness. With a quick twist, I wrapped the cord around his throat. He choked and spit before I even began tightening it.

"Lights out, pansy-ass traitor."

33

Everything was either falling apart or coming together. That thought had Rebecca's foot heavy on the accelerator. The closer she got to home, the more impatient she felt. She'd landed almost an hour ago and had turned her phone back on to see that she had no missed calls.

Not wanting to wait a moment longer, she'd jumped in her cruiser. Talking to Hoyt in person would be easier anyway, and she didn't want to interrupt him if he was still in the middle of his interrogation. The bridge came into sight, and she pressed the accelerator again. Once she reached the halfway point, she was back in her own county, a speeding ticket no longer an issue.

Her phone rang. She pressed the button to put it on Bluetooth. "This is West."

"Hey, Boss, you close?"

"Yeah, I'm coming over the bridge now. Do you have an update?"

"I do, and it's a doozy. You ready for this?"

Rebecca frowned as she turned a sour eye toward the

phone, as if Hoyt could see her. Why did people keep asking if she was ready for things? "Spill it, Frost."

"Landon Hannity is Mitchell Longfellow's biological son. That's why Mitchy was at that party. It wasn't to see Chester Able. It was to convince his son to give up his druggy ways. He still insists he has no idea who Able is, and he never spoke to him. He claimed it was his son calling him from Able's phone. Longfellow had that boy tucked so far inside the closet, he wasn't even allowed to call his dad on the same phone too often."

For a few beats, Rebecca tried to figure out what Hannity's sexuality had to do with anything. "Huh?"

"Of course, Longfellow has so many skeletons in his closet, it wouldn't surprise me to find even more illegitimate kids in there."

She nearly laughed as she caught on to what he'd really meant.

"Did he say why he was at that drug party?"

"He claims he was there to get his son out of it. And he said his son was no longer an addict, so take that as you will."

"Do we have anything to disprove that yet?"

There was a long pause. "Well, no, actually. Autopsy hasn't started."

Rebecca nodded, not sure how they should be looking at this case. "Call Bailey and ask her if she can also get a hair sample from both Overbay and Hannity and run a drug panel on them."

"Hair?"

"Yeah, that's going to show us if they were addicts or just used it for parties. That'll tell us a lot more about who they are than what we've learned from their fathers."

"Will do. Hold on, Viviane has something for us."

Rebecca only had to wait a few seconds.

"Hey, Boss, don't bother heading to the station. Go to the hospital in Coastal Ridge instead."

Dread ran through her as she thought about any number of things that could've gone wrong. "Has Able's condition changed?"

"It has. He's awake and asking to speak to you."

A grin split her face, and she flipped on her lights. "Tell them I'm on my way."

Rebecca slammed on the brakes and wrenched the steering wheel, spinning her cruiser into a graceful U-turn. Finally, they were going to get some real answers.

THE TWO TROOPERS stationed at the hospital entrance waved Rebecca through as she flashed her badge. She didn't recognize them, so she hadn't expected them to recognize her. Someone must've let them know she was on her way.

Jogging, she made it to the room where two more troopers were watching everything with eagle eyes. As she stepped through the door, she spotted Chester Able sitting up in bed. He was drinking water from a straw while Ethan, the nurse Rebecca had encountered earlier, held the cup for him. A series of tight stitches curved along his jawline and up his cheek. The bullet wound would leave a nasty scar.

Not unlike our assassin's scar.

Dr. Stuard was writing in a chart. She glanced over as Rebecca walked in, giving her a little nod.

That caught Able's attention, and his eyes lit up when they landed on her. He pushed the cup away. "Sheriff, I need...confess. Can't meet...maker with...sins on my conscience." His voice was rough and cracked, but he refused the water as it was held in front of him again.

"Mr. Able, before you speak, I need to inform you of your

rights." Rebecca pulled out her phone and activated her recording app. She listed the date, time, and people present. From memory, she recited his Mirandas. "Knowing these rights, Mr. Able, do you wish to proceed?"

He nodded and tried to sit up higher.

"You need to tell me out loud."

"Yes. Waive...rights." Able struggled to stay balanced in his new position against his pillows and slipped instead. He cried out in pain.

"Careful now. Take it slow and easy. We'll use the bed so you can sit up." Dr. Stuard nodded at the nurse, and Ethan started making adjustments. "Sheriff, you can stay and talk with him. But he's still weak. I'll be monitoring his vitals outside. If anything goes wrong, you'll be asked to leave."

"I didn't come here to undo all your hard work, Doc. Just want to make sure our victim here knows he's got the cops on his side." Rebecca moved closer to Able's bed.

"Please, Sheriff, you have...listen to me. They told me it's...Monday, and...it's dark. The deal's going down soon. You need to be there."

Rebecca tapped the nurse on the arm and pointed at the door. She didn't want Ethan hearing anything Able had to say about his job. He gave her a tiny nod and left. "What's going down?" She swung the door shut most of the way, leaving just a crack to make sure she could hear if anyone approached.

"The next deal!" Able tried to lean forward again but stopped and winced in pain. He cupped a hand to his jaw.

She couldn't imagine how much it hurt him to talk. Good drugs probably helped.

"Your doctor said to sit still. You don't want to move your head around too much. And you really don't want to jostle that arm." Rebecca pointed to the phone on the tray by his bedside. "I can hear you just fine. You just need to talk and take it easy. Okay? I wouldn't want your doctor to get angry with me." She gave him a friendly smile and a pat on the shoulder.

"My arm?" He glanced at his hand wrapped in a thick layer of gauze, immobilized by a splint, and strapped to the bed. He shook his head. "Can't feel it. He shot me when I was crossing myself. If I hadn't prayed...I'd be dead right now. Never had a prayer answered so fast in my life. Or ever."

Neither had Rebecca, but she wasn't worried about that right now. "Tell me what happened to you." She shifted closer, hoping it would stop him from moving around so much.

"Me and Landon and Freddie were making the run... thirty bricks of cocaine...just like we did every week. Everything was going fine. Right on time. We've been doing this for months, and we'd gotten it all down pat. We were at... meeting spot and settled in to wait for the pickup. Just a normal day at work."

He stopped and made several dry gulping sounds, his throat sticking audibly each time. Rebecca picked up the cup and twisted the straw to reach his lips. "Here."

He sucked the water down, then shook his head when he was finished. "I have to hurry. Running out of time."

"Go ahead, then." She stayed at his side, ready to offer him more water if it would keep him talking.

"I didn't even see it happen." He cupped his jaw a bit tighter, as if the support made it easier to speak. "I was on the top deck because Landon left his post. That's where we kept a watch for other boats. Never thought we'd need to look out for people. Then I heard yelling, scuffling, from down below. I looked down and I could see Landon and Freddie on the deck." Tears pooled in his eyes. "Freddie was new to this. It was a gig to him. Not even a full-time job like Landon and me. Landon wanted to make a name for himself, start his own business, get out of his dad's shadow. You know?"

"And who is Landon's father?"

"He said he was the treasurer of your island. Mitchell Longfellow. Landon was tired of his bio dad constantly trying to control him with money and his title."

"Okay, please continue."

Able's arm twitched, and he stared at it in confusion. "It won't move." He wiped his eyes with his left hand instead. "Those guys must've paddled up to the boat in one of those rubber dinghies or those inflatable things."

"How many men were there?"

He rubbed his head, as if he could pull the number physically out of his brain. "Five? Maybe?" He winced and cupped his jaw again. "Maybe seven or eight? It felt like they were everywhere."

"And where was your boat exactly?"

"We weren't close to shore."

So much for exactly.

"The shore of…?" she prompted.

Able hesitated. His need to confess seemed to be waning. Rebecca wondered if the reality of his situation was catching up to him. But he continued. "Little Quell Island. We were all looking in the direction the buyers usually came from. Guess that was the wrong direction. Those guys rowed up behind us and climbed aboard. They took us down before we even knew anything was going on. Just, boom, guys swarming all over the boat."

"How did they manage to sneak up on you? Where exactly were you anchored?"

"We were just outside the cove on Little Quell Island, in open water. But there's a little cave-like canopy made of trees near the shore. That's where they came from. Had to. It's the best place to ambush us. It's the only place on the island to hide. Everything else is dunes. They had to be in there before we even got there."

Rebecca was doing her best to put together his rambling recollections. "Were they the buyers?"

"No. I didn't recognize them. They had to be outsiders because they wanted to know who our supplier was. That was all they wanted. That's all they still want. That guy…"

"Which guy?"

Able frowned at her. "The guy who tried to kill me again."

"The guy with the scar on his forehead?"

Able nodded. "He said…he said I needed to tell him my suppliers."

"Did you?"

"No, he would've killed me."

Rebecca tried to keep her tone gentle, not wanting to get him too far off track. "He did try to kill you."

"Only after he realized I wouldn't talk. He asked me a few times. Then he got sick of me, said he'd get the information another way, and to say hello to my friends in Hell. I can't remember what happened next."

A shooting in a hospital, Rebecca thought grimly.

"What do these guys want?" she asked.

"They want to cut us out."

"*Us* being the Yacht Club."

He didn't answer that directly. "Poor Landon told him we were just couriers. He didn't know who we got the packages from. That wasn't good enough."

Able's face crumpled as if he was about to cry. "They shot Freddie in the chest. Then they just picked him up and tossed him in the water. They grilled him first, but he didn't know who our dealer was. I was the only one who knew. This was my job. They were just my crew. Landon was my skipper, Freddie was my backup, but I was the one in charge."

She leaned forward, resting her forearms on her knees. "You're couriers...for who?"

"Sorry, Sheriff. I'm not telling you that. I'm scared of the men who did this." He nodded to his injured arm. "But I'm scared of my suppliers too. It's not worth my life to tell you."

Rebecca wanted to remind him that prison wasn't exactly comfortable, either, but she held her comment. She needed his information and didn't want to shut him up.

Able smoothed the sheets under his hand, refusing to meet her eyes. "They didn't turn on me, you know...Freddie and Landon. Never even said I was there. Both of them protected me. A worthless piece-of-shit drug dealer. Even looking down the barrel of a gun, they didn't out me. They died for me instead. I was going to jump, try to get away. Then those men caught me and demanded I give up my supplier. I wouldn't give them the name either. Nothing personal."

Rebecca held her silence, letting him tell his story his way.

"The people I work for, they don't mess around, but they also don't put their name out there. Any names I'd give you would be aliases, anyway, I'm sure. I've always done blind pickup and drops with them. Probably so cartel hijackers can't get their identities."

"You think these guys were cartel?"

He huffed a humorless laugh. "There've been rumors for months now of hostile relations on these waters. So yeah, I think they're cartel. The hijackers gave me the same treatment they gave Landon and Freddie. Shot me, pitched me overboard, and left me to the sharks and the tides."

That explained at least a little bit of what happened to them. But it also left a lot of questions. "If you make the run every week, why would there be another deal tonight?"

"We're just one of the crews that make this supply run. There're two, sometimes three runs every week to the same guys. They move a lot of product." He took a shaky breath. "I'm guessing this guy is hoping he'll have a second chance to get our supplier's name from one of the other crews making the runs. They were so casual about killing us. They had to have a backup plan. Right? If they hit us and we didn't talk, surely they'll go after the next team tonight." His breath sped up.

Rebecca nodded to calm him down. "Maybe. It'd make sense that if he didn't get the information from you three, he would go after another team." She left off that the hijackers might also be killing all the couriers because that would solve the territory problem too. Perhaps that was plan B.

"What's your supply route? Where do you start, and what route do you take?"

"We load up in Chesapeake. Then we hit our meetup point near Little Quell Island. Once the handover's done, we swing down to Duck to pass off the money there. After that, we usually just take our time coming back. That makes us look more legit, ya get me? We're just some rich douchebags who sail up and down the coast every week looking for pussy and fun."

And they'd been doing it for so long that no one had ever suspected them. Or if anyone had noticed anything, they'd most likely been paid to look the other way.

"So you were the one who made the video of Frederick using drugs and having sex with prostitutes?"

Able blushed and nodded uncomfortably. "Yeah, that was me." He rubbed the back of his neck. "I managed to get a bit of Landon's dad in there, too, since Landon was my skipper. It's always good to have some insurance. So I created the blackmail video."

"Who'd you sell it to? Senator Overbay magically got a copy."

Able paused. "I sent it…to my, um, boss."

"Your boss got a name?"

"Not that I'm going to give you." Able's eyes watered, but Rebecca couldn't tell if it was from pain or fear.

Chester Able wasn't a criminal mastermind. Sending the blackmail video wouldn't have benefitted him. However, Rebecca could think of one group that would love to have a blackmail video of a senator's son involved in a sexed-up drug fest. "Do you work for the Yacht Club?"

He stared at her, and Rebecca sensed him debating his answer.

"Do I look like I could afford to be part of some boat club?" But even as he spoke, he gave the slightest of nods. A nod couldn't be recorded.

This was the biggest admission of the Yacht Club's actual existence Rebecca was going to get from someone on the inside. She could work with it. Perhaps WITSEC could sway him. "I'd have to talk to people with more authority than me, but we might be able to offer you witness protection if you could give us some actionable information."

Able just looked down at his bedsheets.

"What time is the deal supposed to go down tonight?"

"Two. Same as every night. But on the night we were attacked, the hijackers got there before us, and we were there at just past one. I don't know who those guys are. I've never seen them before. I know how you cops work. Without a good description, you can't do shit. Did you even find Landon's boat?"

Even though she was sure it would rile Able up again, Rebecca answered truthfully. "We didn't. He wasn't around to report it stolen. Can you describe it? Maybe we still have a chance. Then we'll have the crime scene too."

He shook his head, and the message was clear—he wasn't giving her names she didn't already know.

Rebecca swallowed a lump of frustration. After he healed,

Chester Able was headed to jail for drug possession and distribution, no question. She knew he wouldn't risk getting killed behind bars by giving too many specifics.

"Did you...did you at least find their bodies?"

"We did manage that. And we got the slug out of your jaw. Now that we have those, we'll have ballistics to match. Did the same man who shot you also shoot your friends?"

Able nodded, and she noticed a tiny wince of pain. "I think so. He was the only one holding a gun, at least. But what if he just tossed the gun in the ocean once he was done? Then you'd have nothing to compare it to."

"What about the boat you were on? Can you tell us the make and model? We haven't found any abandoned boats, and if it had been left at Little Quell Island, then we'd have seen it by now. Did the boat have a name?"

He hesitated. "Um..."

"Whoever hijacked you stole the boat. Give me something."

"Fine. It was the *Clam Strips*. She's a real beauty. I hope you find her."

Rebecca wrote down the name.

"Do you have any idea where Landon got that kind of money for his yacht?"

"Not a clue. I don't think he was raking in enough from his dad to afford it. My best guess is he was doing more drug running on the side. Some big scores where he didn't need to split the proceeds."

Rebecca knew one group of locals who had the resources and willingness to buy a drug runner a nice boat. The Yacht Club had more than a few members who might even have donated an older-model boat, considering it an investment. Looked like the Yacht Club had expanded a little too close to cartel territory. Or the cartel was expanding its reach.

Great. Now we have a turf war.

"You're right, Chester. Finding the boat may not do us any good, even if we can track it down. Ballistics will probably also be useless. The guys you described sound like pros. And professionals don't hold onto their guns after the job is done."

He nodded once. "I know."

Rebecca held Able's gaze for a moment and gave it a shot. "You want to tell me who your suppliers are? How many total crews there are? Who on the island is involved?"

He shook his head. "I can't."

She glanced at the clock on the wall. "It's nine now." We've got just enough time to get things situated. Then we can get out there and set up a couple ambushes of our own.

"Please. Yes. I couldn't save Landon and Freddie, but at least we can get their killer."

"We'll do our best." Rebecca moved away from Able's hospital bed. Three hours was not a lot of time to put together an ambush on a tiny island, but it was their only shot.

34

Rebecca inspected the personnel staged around her. She had, once again, called in all hands on deck. "We don't have time for beating around the bush, so let me get right to it, everyone."

Locke and Viviane, who were standing near the back of the group, gave short nods. Hoyt rotated his shoulders, having an idea of what was going on as he leaned back in his chair. Darian sat placidly, ready for whatever came his way. Greg was at his desk, working through a crossword puzzle covered in smears, as he kept changing his answers.

And Rhonda was leaning on the table next to Rebecca, the coffee pot between them. Both women, knowing what the night held, were fueling up.

"We've got a small gang, roughly five to eight men, of drug dealers who are going to be making a run on Little Quell Island. We think they're going to take down the couriers so they can get a direct line to the supply. These are the men who were responsible for the deaths of Frederick Overbay and Landon Hannity, and the attempted murder of

Chester Able. We need to be in place and ready within two hours." Rebecca motioned to Rhonda.

A disturbance in the lobby caught everyone's attention, and Ryker craned his neck around the corner. "Is my timing perfect? Or awful?" The hopeful smile on his face as he peered into the bullpen tugged at Rebecca's heart. His expression faltered as he got a good look at the serious expressions on everyone's faces.

Rebecca moved over to the door that separated the lobby from the bullpen so they could talk without every word being overheard.

"It's pretty bad." She knew time wasn't on their side, no matter how much she wanted to run off with Ryker right now.

"I can see that. What's going on?"

She shrugged, not sure how to cushion what she was about to tell him. Ryker had been her sounding board since her first case here. Still, he wasn't law enforcement. "We got intel there's a drug deal about to happen nearby with the POI from our current case, so we're going to get there early and scoop them up as they land. We've got the drop on them."

"You're heading out on a drug bust?" He frowned, and she saw the worry flicker on and off as he tried to decide how dangerous that could be.

Rebecca intentionally downplayed the risks. Her mind needed to be focused on the mission, and she didn't have time to fret over whether Ryker was worried about her safety.

"Yup, just a drug bust. Standard. Rhonda's securing us a boat to get there. Then we'll stare at the stars for the next two hours or so, pick up the dealers, and get a ride back with the state police again." She did her best to make this sound as simple as possible.

He lifted a bag he'd been clutching in his hand. "Well, I brought you a snack, just in case you had to work late."

Rebecca's heart melted into goo and puddled around her stomach, which growled loudly. "I love you too." Heat rushed into her cheeks as he dropped the bag.

He quickly scooped it up again. "Do...were you talking to me or to the food?"

Her blush deepened until she could nearly see the glow radiating off her cheeks.

Rebecca had a moment she could take it back, play it off, or brush it aside. She hadn't meant to say it. That didn't mean it wasn't true. There was more than one way to prove love for someone. Driving out at nearly midnight to make sure that person had food while not trying to interfere with their work said it loud and clear, and she couldn't help but respond to it. There was no way she was going to take it back now.

"I was talking to you."

"Good." His eyes lit up, and his smile was as sweet as a homecoming. "Because I love you, too, Rebecca West. I won't embarrass you in front of your crew, though. So just take the snack and think of each bite as a kiss from me."

Rebecca took the bag from him, then leaned across the half door. "Just a quick taste first. And my deputies know when to keep their mouths shut." She leaned forward and kissed him. Everything that had happened that day washed away, and all thoughts of what she was supposed to be doing went up in smoke as his hand slid around the back of her head.

When the kiss intensified long enough to make her toes tingle and her hand clutch onto his shirt collar, the screaming and hooting from the bullpen was the only thing that brought her back to reality.

Ryker pulled back, keeping his eyes locked on hers. "Be

safe tonight. Call me when you get off, and we can pick up where we left off."

"That can't happen soon enough," she whispered against his lips, then she kissed him one more time.

When Rebecca turned back around, Greg was staring at her from across his puzzle, the only one bold enough to make eye contact. She carried her bag from Ryker back over to the coffee pot and set it on the table near where Rhonda was staring intently into her mug.

Rebecca faced the group, pretending nothing had happened, and cleared her throat. "Thanks to Chester Able, we've learned the name of Landon Hannity's boat is the *Clam Strips*. Try to ignore it. We're not sure if the men who killed Landon are still using it or not. But that's one more thing to keep an eye out for."

Darian nodded. "Yes, sir."

Glancing at her deputies, she found most of the smirks had left their faces. They were all business now, just as they needed to be.

"Rhonda, can you hook us up with a boat? We usually ask our guy, Silas, but his little speedboat wouldn't be enough for this job."

"Of course. Give me a few minutes to make some calls. We should have some suitable resources in the area."

Darian stood up to get Rebecca's attention. "We should be loaded for bear. Getting in the middle of a drug deal is always messy."

"Everyone needs to take at least one handgun and a rifle or shotgun as well. I'm taking both my handguns. Bring all the Saigas."

Rebecca reached for her keys, then realized she'd left them with her senior deputy when she went out of town.

Darian waggled his fingers at Hoyt. "Toss me the keys, and I'll get everything."

Hoyt handed them over, and Viviane and Locke went with Darian to the weapons locker built into the wall of the hallway opposite her office door.

"As for the people, it'll be Locke, Darian, Hoyt, and me. We're going to be playing lookout tonight. As soon as we see anyone approaching the drop-off point, we call it in."

"I'll make sure we've pulled back all our boats in the area so the target doesn't get spooked by our presence." Rhonda took out her phone to make a call.

Viviane spun on Rebecca, mouth open and ready to protest, her eyes narrowed.

Rebecca knew what she was going to say and cut her off. "Viviane, I need you here, handling the radio and ready to call in backup if we need. We don't know what we might face out there and we have to prepare for all contingencies as best we can. If the radio fails, we might end up having to use our phones. In which case, we'll need to have one number we all know and can call that'll be answered swiftly...and by someone who knows what we're doing. There's no way around it. I need you here."

Pressing her lips together, Viviane wordlessly went to help Darian with the firearms. Rebecca wondered if she'd get an earful about this later. Friend to friend, of course.

She tucked three spare 1911 magazines, all she had, into her pouch.

Rhonda surveyed the group. "I've got two of our Marine Unit boats coming out, plus a boat for your group. They should be here in about five minutes. We're going to be anchored along the northern edge of Shadow Island. Our Marine SWAT group is patrolling the perimeter of the island, so they should be able to respond as needed once we identify a target. The Coast Guard'll be backing us up, waiting on our call near the mainland. We've also got a helicopter on standby. As soon as you guys call it in, we'll be there within minutes."

Locke came back with three shotguns slung over his shoulder and an AR-15 in his hand. Rebecca waved her fingers at him in a *gimme* gesture. Locke passed over a Saiga 12-gauge shotgun, then frowned at Rhonda.

She waved him off. "No, thanks. I'll load up once I meet up with my guys."

Viviane came out with boxes of ammo lined up in her arms and dropped them on the spare desk with a rattling *thunk*. "Good, because between the shotguns and the hand-guns, we're going to use up most of our stock."

Everyone began passing around magazines and getting them loaded. Darian tossed Rebecca two spare magazines for her shotgun, and Hoyt passed her a box of shells before taking the AR-15 from Locke.

"Once we're on Little Quell Island, we'll need to hide. There's a natural hut-like collection of trees that Hoyt and I saw when we went out there once. The rest of you might know about it as well. Able suspects that's where the crew who attacked him were hiding. I believe he's correct, since that's honestly the only place on the island to hide. Because it's made from living trees, we can use it as a blind, looking out through the branches."

Darian nodded. "I'm familiar, sir."

Rebecca slid the box open with her thumb and started loading.

"Like I said earlier, we don't know what might happen out there, so we need to prepare for any eventuality. Every-one, set your phones to silent. We need to stay hidden until we see the hijackers." She noted then that Locke hadn't moved off yet. "Did you have a question, Deputy Locke?"

Locke hesitated, staring at the two weapons he was hold-ing, then at Rebecca. "You said this had something to do with

Chester Able, the man who was found on the beach mostly dead Saturday morning?" Locke set down one gun and started fiddling with the other.

The junior deputy sounded guilty, and as far as Rebecca knew, he'd done nothing wrong on this case. In fact, she thought he'd been doing better than normal, been more focused than usual. That made her even more uneasy. "Yes. It was Chester Able who survived the attack and gave us this information." She finished inserting the eleventh shell in her shotgun magazine and racked it into the chamber, then dropped the magazine once more and added the final shell.

Locke nodded, clenching his jaw. "Um, Sheriff West, I think I need to tell you something."

The muscles in Rebecca's shoulders and back tightened. Locke had never asked to speak to her before. In fact, he'd gone out of his way to avoid her when he could. She felt her face go stony as she strapped the last spare magazine onto her belt. "Then I suggest, Deputy Locke, that you go ahead and tell me."

She didn't have time for this shit and wanted it over with as quickly as possible. Grabbing a single-point sling from the pile Darian had brought, she clipped it to the shotgun, threw the loop over her head, and tucked it under her shoulder so it could swing easily and not be in her way.

Locke shuffled his feet, staring at the floor, his hands, the desk, anything but her. "I think we should discuss this in private." He finally raised his eyes, meeting her gaze for only a moment before dropping them again. "Sheriff, I think I really fucked up."

Rebecca gave a harsh nod, all but grinding her teeth. "Fine." She led him out of the bullpen. She stopped halfway to her office and spun on him. "This is enough privacy. Tell me what you need to tell me. Now."

Locke, who'd been right on her heels, dithered to a halt.

He ran a hand over the patchy beard he'd been trying to regrow. "Do you remember when I showed up after shaving my beard?"

She nodded and crossed her arms over her chest, causing the stock of the shotgun to hang down across her belly. "I remember."

"I didn't do it to myself. My friends who did it…at least, I thought they were my friends…showed up a couple days ago. I thought they were coming back to apologize. It happened at a party, we were all drunk, they were mad because I wouldn't talk about work."

"Are these the same people who gave you the black eye and split lip the same night they shaved you?"

He turned bright red and gave the barest of nods.

At the time, she'd been startled at his sudden change, but so much had happened that night, and they'd both ended up in the hospital with head wounds just after, that she'd mostly forgotten it. Looking back now, she realized that had been a mistake on her part, ignoring an attack on one of her men. Even if he was a pain in the ass, he was still a law enforcement officer under her command, and she should have followed up with him about it.

"That doesn't sound very friendly to me. It sounds more like they were trying to hurt and humiliate you." Rebecca scrutinized the forty-one-year-old deputy, noting not for the first time how immature he could be when it came to his personal life.

"It's not like that. Uh, we just sometimes get out of hand when we're messing around." Locke backtracked immediately, and she noted how he jumped to defend them, as if on reflex.

That was a common reaction from someone who was being bullied or abused—protecting their aggressors. Rebecca had expected a lot of things when she led Locke down the hallway, but feeling sympathy for him was not one of them. Still, there wasn't enough time for her to explain that he deserved better friends. All she could do now was make a mental note to do so later.

"We'll set that aside for now. What's so important you had to bring it up now?"

Locke took a short, deep breath. "They told me 'keep the trash off the beach' and that if any of it washes ashore, to make sure I 'push it back out into the water.' That's what they said. At the time, I thought they were making fun of me. Calling me a trash collector or beach sweeper or something. Now I'm wondering, though. They've never said anything like that before."

That sounded ominous. "When did they tell you that? And what did you do?"

He shook his head. "I didn't do anything, Sheriff. I swear it. I wasn't anywhere near a beach until Hudson called me to come help him." Locke looked her in the eye. "Saturday morning. It was real early, too, before dawn. I thought they came over to my place to apologize, because they never get up that early for anything that isn't important. Hours later, a man washed up on the shore." He scrubbed a hand over his face. "They're my friends, but I can't believe they didn't know something was up."

After Chester, Freddie, and Landon had been hijacked, it made sense that the Yacht Club wouldn't want evidence of their botched drug running—or the cartel's vengeful presence—to just lie around on the beach for the whole island to see. Bad for business.

Rebecca lowered her voice and took half a step forward. "Are you sure they're actually your friends?" She hadn't been able to help herself. His calling the people who abused, forcefully shaved, and belittled him his friends was too much for her. "I'm going to need the name of the person who told you to keep an eye out on the beach."

"It was Christian Mallard."

Rebecca sighed and squared her shoulders as Locke confirmed her suspicions. "Christian Mallard is a member of the Yacht Club."

He held his hands up defensively and shook his head. "Look, I know they get a bad rap, but that's just because people are jealous of the wealth the Yacht Club people have, so they make up stories about what they're 'probably' doing. I've known these people my whole life. They're not bad guys just because they like to go out and party sometimes."

His defense of the Yacht Club and its members, not just his friends, bothered Rebecca. She couldn't afford to have fewer people heading out with her, but it would be suicidal to take a man she couldn't trust. "We're about to head out to take down drug dealers that most likely work for the Yacht Club. Are you telling me you can't be impartial?"

He reared back, offended. "No, of course not."

Rebecca scowled at how quickly he denied his own bias. "You just told me they might have asked you to hide a body."

"Might!" Locke made a fist, as if he could cling to that word. "My buddies won't be there. I know that. Even if it ended up being them, I would still arrest them. If they're involved in this...they go down. In order to be a law enforcement officer, I need to enforce the law. Not just help out my friends. Victims and the families of victims deserve justice. That's why I'm telling you all this."

Rebecca wasn't sure where that last part came from, but he did seem serious about it. And despite every bad feeling she had about Locke, she'd never caught him intentionally sabotaging anything.

In fact, he'd even stood shoulder to shoulder with her while going after Kevin Garland. His comment about helping out his friends stuck in her craw, though. Was Locke part of Shadow's conspiracy? There simply wasn't time to deal with this now, and being distracted before going out was a bad plan too.

"Then let's stop wasting time and go catch some criminals."

35

I dug my compact binoculars out of my pocket, turning them toward Shadow Island, where I watched as a medium-sized boat, loaded with deputies, left the shore.

The bonus of having a tight-knit crew of people who could take commands was that I had eyes and ears everywhere. For the past twenty-four hours, one crew member or another had been tracking police movements across Shadow Island. Since Longfellow was no longer available, I had to take matters into my own hands.

Lo and behold, the good sheriff had headed off to the hospital where Chester Able, the current bane of my existence, was still alive. When Chip came back with that news, I knew Able had talked. There wasn't a doubt in my mind that Able, the dumb son of a bitch, had mentioned the rendezvous scheduled for tonight. The bastard had probably compromised everything.

We'd been sitting here, idle, for a couple hours now, resting up for big happenings tonight. Our ride had dropped us off and returned to the marina. A few of my men were busy pumping up our inflatable rafts for the evening's festivities. Over the years, I'd learned motors drew attention, so I focused on coming in slow and silent.

Plus, rowing was better for the back muscles.

I scanned the ocean surface, catching the telltale pale, churned-up wake created by a propeller.

Guess only one of us is smart enough not to use a motor. Tsk, tsk.

The boat I was observing was too small to be an armed Coast Guard boat. From the height of it, I was betting it was someone's fishing boat. It only came into view for a short time as it crested the waves and became backlit by the lights from the town. Once past, it faded into the dark of the night. They were running without lights. That meant one of two things.

"Either that's our runner coming in very early, or the sheriff and her men are on their way out here." I folded my binoculars and tucked them into my pocket.

"The sheriff?"

I glanced over at Tweety. The moon was out and bright enough, but we were already set up under the matted trees. Half of us were wearing camo, so it wasn't easy to pick everyone out of the shadows.

There was a hint of worry in his voice. "Is he going to mess up our plans?"

"This sheriff is a she. And it looks like she will be part of our plans tonight."

There was a shuffling of feet all around as my men shifted on the layers of dead plants that made up most of Little Quell Island since the hurricane had shredded it. Their jumpiness could've been from anxiety or eagerness at the idea of going up against the cops. It was anybody's guess at this point.

"She thinks she's coming out here to ambush us. But she's got another thing coming." That got a round of low chuckles. "We're going to kill two birds with one stone. We're going to clear out the sheriff's department and intercept the deal going down tonight, then head off into the great blue yonder. Why do you think I brought so many of you tonight? Lots to do."

We were already set up and ready to take on anyone who came our way. And we'd made sure to properly plan things so we could take our time tonight. No one would be interrupting us. Once I took down the sheriff and the deputies loyal to her and the couriers for Longfellow's supplier, the payout was going to be huge. It would also open up this area for Amado.

Thank you, Longfellow.

I took a moment to really see the view around me instead of just inspecting it for dangers and possibilities. Shadow Island was a crap hole, but plenty of places around it were larger and better suited to someone like me. It'd be easy pickings to move into the power vacuum left behind in this area once the sheriff was gone. I might even be able to settle down.

"Go to the secondary locations. More than likely, once they land, they'll head straight to the hut we used last time." I lifted the radio and cell phone jammers high enough that my crew of fifteen could see them, and they turned theirs on. Little red lights shined merrily in the dark. "We can take our time wiping them out."

36

"How long until we're in position?" Rhonda walked the deck of the Virginia Marine Police speedboat. She'd been on plenty of boats over the years but had never been good at judging location out on the water like this. With the moon shining strong in the clear night sky, everything was either too dark or too bright.

The lights of Shadow Island were closer, she knew, but they appeared the same distance away as the brighter lights of the larger towns on the mainland behind it as they all blended together. It was like floating in a carnival funhouse, as far as she was concerned.

The captain checked his instruments. "Another five minutes."

Their plan was to swing up the east side of Shadow Island, then get far enough away from both islands to not be easily seen while maintaining a direct line to reach their target as soon as they were signaled.

"Let's get settled in for the wait, then." Rhonda picked up her binoculars. "Which way is Little Quell Island?"

One of the officers tapped her on the shoulder and

pointed. "You probably won't be able to see anything at this distance. It'll be coming into view just over there."

She followed his arm, swinging the binoculars along. Her view ran over Shadow Island, and she adjusted the focus. Little Quell Island would be farther away, but since they weren't sure where the boat was coming from, she wanted to scope out everything she could while she had the chance.

Most boats were docked at this hour, tied up and dark. The glow coming up on her left let her know that she was moving toward a section that wasn't closed for the night.

Tall, regal luxury yachts came into view. They were lined up neatly. A few of them had people on the decks, talking, drinking...there even seemed to be a few parties happening. This had to be the high-end marina she'd heard so much about, where the rich and famous spent their summers.

One was out of line, so it caught her eye. Instead of being nestled in a numbered dock, it was tied to the end of it. The stern was drifting, showing it only had the ropes along the bow secured.

"Someone had a bit too much to drink tonight."

"What was that?"

Rhonda waved the officer off. Talking to herself had always been a habit. Her gaze casually ran over the name on the transom above the swimming platform. She jerked, straightening up, then leaned forward to read it again.

She hadn't misread. The yacht she was looking at was the *Clam Strips*. Landon Hannity's boat that had been missing since he was murdered.

"Pull into the marina." Rhonda scanned over the decks, looking for signs that anyone was on board. The boat rocked under her feet as it started to turn.

"What do you see?" The officer leaned next to her, pulling up his own binoculars.

"Our target." She leaned next to his shoulder and pointed

so he could follow her arm out. "They're docked here, probably waiting for the right time to head to Little Quell Island. We can take them before they even get underway if we move fast enough."

The officer by her side nodded, then ran off to spread the word on the change of plans. The boat had a single light on in the cabin, and Rhonda could see a few shadows moving around inside. It was also docked among other boats that didn't have any occupants in sight.

Rhonda picked up her radio and called in ground units. With how this was laid out, and where she knew everyone was at this moment, they could perform a perfect pincer maneuver with the two boats, the dozen cruisers, and the two dozen troopers she had on standby.

This was turning out better than she could've hoped for. She could board the boat, smoke out the crew, and finally take control of their primary crime scene and the killers in one swift operation. It might even be possible to do it with no loss of life.

That was her idea of a perfect night—one where no one had to die.

REBECCA STEPPED out of the little cabin on the boat where they'd all stayed out of sight during the trip as Greg pulled the staties' boat up next to the island. He pointed over his shoulder to Shadow Island. "Here ya go, Sheriff. Did you want me to hang around the west coast in case you need a pickup?"

She looked around, but there was nothing to see. The full moon lit up the ocean. Its light faded out along the coast from the light pollution of large cities, but out here, it cast a cool blue glow over everything.

"No, we don't want to spook anyone. Go ahead and head back to town. We'll meet up with you later. Just keep your radio on in case we need a ride back early." She stepped out the door and made her way to the swim platform on the stern. The others filed after her. He'd drifted the boat up within a few feet of the sand. Though Rebecca found pulling in this close alarming, Greg had said the boat could handle water just a couple of feet deep, and she trusted him.

"Sounds good. Happy hunting."

Rebecca hopped off the boat and onto the tiny shore, the only one the entire island had. Once everyone else had followed, the engines revved up again, and the boat pulled away, leaving them alone and hopefully unseen.

Rebecca's radio crackled to life. "Sheriff West, this is Special Agent Lettinger, do you read me, over?"

"Read you loud and clear. Over."

"We've spotted the *Clam Strips* at the Seaview Marina. We are preparing to board the ship. Please—"

Static filled the air.

Shit.

"Lettinger, transmission lost. Please repeat, over." Nothing but static came back.

Rebecca scanned the water for Greg's boat, but he was gone. She then surveyed her group, all three awaiting her decision. "Well, we may've run out here for nothing. But let's go ahead and take cover and wait to hear the all-clear signal."

The rest of the island was covered in trees that grew down to just above the water and made it impossible to approach. She glanced up and down the minuscule beach, looking for any sign they weren't alone. There was nothing there—not a boat, not a raft, not a piece of driftwood. Only plants struggled to grow upright in the constant breeze from the ocean. It looked the same as it had the last time she'd been here.

Hoyt moved up beside her. "Make sure whoever brings up the rear erases our footprints."

"It's off this way, right?" Rebecca peered at the distant foliage. Even if everything looked the same, she'd only visited once, that time during daylight.

"Yup." He gestured to the west, his other hand resting loosely on the rifle at his waist, hanging from a two-point sling.

"Let's get there and under cover. We're running low on time."

They headed out with Darian and Locke following.

They'd been running dark, so none of them needed to wait while their eyes adjusted to the shadows. They walked in a line with Locke doing a bit of a shuffling dance at the rear to scuff the ground and cover their tracks. That only lasted a few steps as the sand soon gave way to a carpeting of bent grasses and twisted, broken trees.

Even if an army walked over the matted foliage, it would be nearly impossible to find any tracks now. The deeper they moved into the island, the more secure Rebecca felt. Everything was working just as planned.

The little naturally occurring hut—where several scraggly trees had fallen against each other and continued to grow that way—came into view.

She had to duck to get inside then shift to the side so the others could come in as well. "Keep an eye out. We don't know which direction they'll be coming from."

"More like keep an ear out. We should be able to hear their engines as they approach. Even if they're using oars, we should hear them moving through the water." Darian tilted his head, indicating the beach they'd just left. It was the only place to come ashore, unless they wanted to swim up to the trees and climb out there.

They were all packed in, with the three men crouching. Rebecca only had to duck her head slightly. One of the few benefits of being the shortest person at work. Darian and Hoyt were stationed near the front and Locke was to her left.

The air was already getting stale from their exhalations. The late summer foliage was thicker than the last time she'd seen it and actually managed to block the view. Still, they had enough room to move around.

However, most of the moonlight was hidden by the thick leaves over their heads and around the sides.

The way the leaves rustled against the branches made a slithering sound, and everything echoed strangely. Tiny sounds became loud, and louder sounds were muffled. Rebecca heard little clicks as insects walked around, alerted by their presence, but the shushing of the waves was completely absent until she shifted closer to the entrance. She kept glancing down, certain this would be the type of habitat that would draw snakes.

Something tickled her hair, and she ducked lower, rolling her eyes up. Her mind was suddenly focused on the knowledge that snakes ate insects and could, in fact, be over their heads and not just around her feet.

There was nothing above her other than drooping leaves and twigs. Still, she crouched to put some space between her and any possible dangling serpents. The last thing she needed was to get startled by a leaf and ruin their ambush.

Darian held his clenched fist up in the air, and she and Hoyt froze. "Did you hear that?" He mouthed the words and tapped his ear. His other hand reached down for the shotgun hanging at his waist.

He and Hoyt slowly turned to face the back of the hut. She realized they must've heard something she couldn't, and the hairs on the back of her neck stood on end.

A stab of anxiety twisted her stomach. She reached up with her left hand, took hold of Locke's wrist, and yanked him down next to her.

"Like fish in a barrel!" The voice of an unseen man came from somewhere on the other side of the hut seconds before the peaceful silence was shredded by gunfire.

They got here before us. Shit!

Locke was already pitching to the side from her hard pull. But he screamed as his wrist jerked in her grip.

Darian dropped like his legs had been yanked out from under him. Hoyt threw himself down at his side then rolled a half turn as bullets kicked up sand where he'd lain.

Bullets tore through the air over their heads. Still, Rebecca reflexively ducked, pulled her Armory 1911, and twisted so Locke wouldn't fall on her. He landed in front of her knees as she spun on the balls of her feet.

"Ugh. That hurts like a bitch." Locke's grumbling sent a wave of relief through Rebecca.

The moonlight was brighter now that Hoyt and Darian weren't blocking it.

Someone started laughing outside, and she shifted her gun muzzle in that direction.

"Die, pigs!"

She fired and, with a choked-out scream, the threat ended.

With ears ringing from the hail of gunfire so close, Rebecca pulled the trigger twice more.

Leaves and branches fell like rain around them, opening the hut's walls. As low as she was, she couldn't bring her shotgun into play without standing up, since it was pinned at her side against the ground.

Through the haze of gun smoke and debris, she saw a row of men positioned like an execution squad—too many to count—firing as quickly as they could without bothering to aim. That was the only thing that saved them from going down in the first barrage.

Their ambush had been a trap.

37

Rebecca emptied her magazine, aiming for every man who came into sight. The thunderous boom of Darian's shotgun joined her. Locke rolled away, struggling to pull his Glock from his holster. She was the only one still on her feet, even if she was crouched over them. But even flat on his back, Hoyt pulled the AR-15 up and dropped two men.

Her fingers went through the motions, dropping her empty magazine and slapping in a fresh one as she tried to shuffle backward.

The ambushers could use the same tactic she had, aiming at the source of the gunfire. In her crouch, she'd take a shot to the legs and then she wouldn't be able to get away at all.

A hand grabbed her vest and tugged it twice—Locke signaling her to get back. He sat up and gave her covering fire.

Twisting to her hands and knees, Rebecca crawled behind him, stopping short of where Hoyt was still firing to cover for Darian, who had his hand on his radio, screaming into it while struggling to fire the shotgun one-handed.

Rebecca pulled her Ruger, which held four more rounds than her 1911.

She tapped Hoyt, signaling him before she started firing with both guns. Locke and Hoyt scrambled away while she covered. Despite her training to shoot with either hand, her right was still faster, and the 1911 emptied first. Locke moved up on the other side of her again as the Ruger also ran out of ammo.

She dropped her magazines to reload.

Then it felt like a mule kicked her shoulder.

The bullet, impeded by her vest, knocked her flat. Before her body had time to react to the pain or the wind whooshing out of her, she used the momentum from the bullet's impact to continue in that direction, doing a backward somersault and landing on her knees behind her men, her left hand empty. The spent Ruger was lost somewhere in the darkness.

A blur of movement happened in that moment.

Locke lunged in front of Rebecca as another shot rang out, dropping him in a heap.

"Locke!"

The deputy stirred and crawled closer to them instead of returning fire, seemingly out of ammo. "I'm good." His voice strained through gritted teeth. He wrapped one hand around the back of his leg, but Rebecca couldn't see the injury in the moving shadows. "I can keep going."

"Move!" Darian was laid flat on his stomach, one empty shotgun magazine beside him. "No radio!" He had to scream to be heard over the gunfire. Thankfully, most of it was from their side now, so the attackers were the ones seeking cover.

Hoyt was pushing himself backward with his feet, shooting from a slightly curled position, his head and shoulders lifted off the ground. Locke slipped around behind him, staying out of his line of fire, but then fell with a scream as his injured leg collapsed under him.

Rebecca dropped onto her elbows and knees.

"Out!" Darian yelled as he darted over to Rebecca's position.

For a terrifying moment, she thought he was trying to shield her just as Locke had done a moment earlier. But Darian grabbed hold of Locke, stood up to a crouch, and flung the man out the entrance and to a semblance of safety, leaving behind a pool of blood on the ground.

Hoyt finally worked his way backward past her, putting her in front again.

Rebecca tapped the earbud she'd worn in the event this happened, digging her phone out of her pocket. She hit the first speed dial and waited for it to ring. Dropping the phone on the ground in front of her, she pulled her own Saiga shotgun around. Nothing but silence came back on the call.

She continued shooting the 1911 at anything that moved until it was empty again, dropping at least one more of their assailants. "Go!"

Despite Darian moving over her, she brought the Saiga to bear. The sound as she fired over and over was enough to rattle all the bones on the left side of her body.

Darian grunted above her and took a step back.

"Clear!" Hoyt yelled from behind.

She dropped her 1911 magazine and pulled her last one. When she heard the AR-15 and a Glock firing again, she flattened herself a bit more, slithered under Darian, and rolled out of the hut and to the side to lean up against a tree trunk.

Movement on her left caught her attention. She lifted the shotgun one-handed and unloaded her final shots. A different shotgun went off behind her, and the man who was trying to flank them went down.

"Fuck you, fucker!" A wave of relief went through

Rebecca when she heard Locke scream at the dead man. Despite the two shots he'd taken and the blood he'd lost, he was rallying.

Rebecca dropped the shotgun so she could slap her last magazine into her 1911. "Last mag."

"Got two!" Darian responded.

"Cover me!"

Darian obliged, firing his shotgun into the tree line at anything that moved.

Now that they were out of the hut, they had a tiny bit more coverage from the trees and the hut's sides.

"Call it in, Locke. Radios are down." Maybe he'd get through where her call hadn't. Rebecca lifted her 1911 and shotgun again, watching for any kind of threat.

She heard him scrambling, trying to do as she said while she covered him.

"Who's hurt?"

Locke's response was immediate. "I'm shot in the leg, but I don't think it's bad."

"I think I'm going fucking deaf." Hoyt snorted and, out of the corner of her eye, she saw him wiggling a finger in his ear.

"I'm peachy." Darian's voice was rough, probably from inhaling so much dirt and gunpowder. "Locke, your arm's bleeding too."

"Oh, yeah. Got hit there too. That's just a scratch, though."

"Rule number one in a firefight...try to stay out of the bullet's way, 'kay?"

Things had been moving so fast and hectic, Rebecca hadn't had time to feel anything. Now that she'd heard from all of them, some of the shock was settling down. Cautious relief ran through her, and she took her first full breath in what felt like hours. She might have inadvertently led her men into an ambush, but at least they'd survived the initial attack.

Each time worry and fear threatened to choke her, she had to battle to push them aside.

They weren't out of the thick of things yet. She turned to Locke. He was sitting about three feet behind her, with his legs splayed. He still had his Saiga in his right hand, and it was up and pointed. His phone was pressed to his ear in his other hand.

He saw her looking and shook his head. "Phone's not ringing. I don't know what's going on."

"That's what happened with mine." Rebecca turned back to the front. There'd been no shots for so long already that she found the time to twist around to get up on her feet. "Fucking hell. Cover me, Hudson."

"Ten-four." Darian knelt, propping his bag in front of himself, either as a shield, a gun prop, or both.

Too much time had passed. Rebecca tried to remember how many men she'd seen. It had to have been more than a dozen. She'd counted five who fell. When she asked how many everyone else got, Darian added two more to her count. Without being able to check the bodies, she couldn't be sure if they were dead or just down.

"Come on, Vi. Pick up, dammit!" Now that her ears weren't ringing quite so badly, Locke's voice seemed thready. She hoped his blood pressure wasn't dropping.

Chuckles from several different voices filtered out from the trees, making Rebecca's blood go cold.

"We're not going to get a signal." She kept her voice to a whisper, twisting around as she tried to find where the laughter was coming from.

Darian apparently heard Locke's weakening voice too. "Frost, take over. Locke needs the med kit." Darian dropped his weapons and started digging in his bag, certain that he would be covered.

"Make it fast, man." Hoyt was on his feet as well, crouched low and swaying back and forth as he kept an eye out.

Darian flung the medical kit onto Locke's lap and resumed digging around inside the bag. "Stop the bleeding."

Locke looked at the kit, then stared at his Saiga, clearly confused about how to handle both things at once.

Rebecca duckwalked to his side, stopping next to the leg he was clutching. She'd spent so long crouched, her leg muscles were starting to cramp. Her shotgun hung from its sling, and she holstered her 1911.

"If I get shot in the back…" She unzipped the pouch.

"I've got your back, Sheriff. I swear it." Locke lifted his weapon to reassure her.

Finding the roll of gauze, she ripped it from its packaging. Sliding her fingers over the bloody flesh, she found the bullet wound dead center of the thick thigh muscle. Hooking a finger into the hole in his pants, she had to yank twice to get it to rip wide enough to stuff the small mass inside. She didn't bother to warn him.

Locke bit back a sound that might've started as a scream. Instead, it came out as a whoosh of air.

She wrapped another roll tight against the wound, then pulled out the rubber tourniquet and wrapped it around his upper thigh. It wasn't pretty, but it would hold the blood inside his body.

"Got it." Rebecca looked up from her bloody work and spotted Darian holding a short, fat, bright-orange pistol.

"Can't jam a flare gun." He pulled the hammer back.

She grinned at his genius work-around. *We'll contact reinforcements one way or another.* Wiping her hands on her pants, she reached for her Saiga again.

At the same moment, there was a rustle in the trees.

Locke fired, splattering the side of her face with gunpowder.

She squinted one eye but raised her weapon at the moving target she could barely make out in the trees.

Hoyt's AR-15 barked rapidly to her right.

Darian turned, raising his arm toward Shadow Island.

Instead of the pop of the flare, there was a bloodcurdling scream.

Rebecca whipped around as Darian's arm dropped.

The flare shot off, barely reaching above the scrubby tree line as Darian collapsed.

Blood coated his vest.

38

"Hudson!"

Rebecca started to scramble to reach him but stopped when Hoyt stepped over and knelt next to Darian. Keeping his eyes forward, Hoyt reached down and helped Darian up, then shot the next man to run out. "They got behind us!"

Following Hoyt's example, Rebecca slipped Locke's shotgun sling over his head and hauled him to his feet. "Can you walk?"

"I can run if you can get us out of here." He stared at her holding a shotgun in each hand.

"Then follow me and watch my back." Swinging the shotguns left to right, she sprayed buckshot through the trees. Screams rang out as she pressed forward, Locke limping behind her. Hoyt fell in with her—Darian's arm over his shoulders—as she continued clearing the path to the beach. She had no idea if there were any men in front of her, but she kept firing regardless.

They cleared the first ten yards, but Rebecca knew the rest of the ambush had to be closing in behind them. She didn't really have a plan, only a concept of one. If they made it to the ocean, that was at least one direction where they couldn't be attacked from.

Her eyes caught movement to the right along the tree line as the beach came into view. She swung a shotgun in that direction and squeezed the trigger. Nothing happened. Rebecca let go of Locke's shotgun, and it fell to her feet. She pulled her 1911 once again. She had a full magazine, so she only had seven shots to fire into the shifting shadows.

Regardless, she pointed and pulled the trigger until the bullets ran out.

A man dropped with a .45 in his chest, and she breathed a sigh of relief.

Then he straightened up and lifted his arm, pointing his handgun at her. She whipped her shotgun around and pulled the trigger. This time, he fell and did not get up.

"Is that all of them?" Locke hopped on one foot, trying to twist in every direction without falling over on a leg that wouldn't support him. She knew the tourniquet could only be used for a short time. It was already cutting off the blood flow to the rest of his leg. They needed to get help, fast.

"No idea. Don't count on it." So far, her spray-and-pray method had worked to keep most of the other ambushers back. No one wanted to get close to someone randomly shooting from the hip like she was. If they did, well, they got what they deserved.

Rebecca knelt in the sand and dropped her empty magazine. Her 1911 was out. "Dammit."

She looked at her people and realized they wouldn't have any ammo for her. They all carried 9mms while she carried a .45.

Hoyt pulled Darian onto the beach, turning to cover the left side as she covered the right.

"Dammit." She inspected her men. They all looked rough as hell.

"You okay, man?" Hoyt lowered Darian so he could sit in the surf.

"Shiiiiiiiiiiiiit, no!" Darian struggled to pull in another lungful of air. "I've got sand in my boots. Fucking hell."

Rebecca smiled at that. He might be beat up, but that wouldn't stop him from busting Hoyt's balls.

"I keep telling you, if you lift your feet up completely instead of dragging them along, that won't happen." Hoyt knelt, casually kicking a clump of wet sand onto the hand Darian was holding himself up with.

"Frost, I...I've got to tell you something. And I mean this, so listen closely."

Hoyt stopped grinning and looked at Darian.

Darian's face was ashen and slick with sweat. His voice came out strangled, and it was clear he was having problems breathing.

"What is it?"

"Fuck you, Hoyt." Darian laughed, then groaned. His elbow buckled, and he nearly toppled over. "Oh, that hurts. Stop making me laugh, you dickhead."

Hoyt chuckled. "That's what you get for being insubordinate to your superiors."

"I have only the...utmost respect for my...superiors." Wobbling, Darian turned to Rebecca, breathing hard. "Isn't that right, West? She's a...fucking badass, and I'm proud to serve under her. Did you see the way she cleared the field, Locke? She's a...badass. Listen to her, she'll...teach you a thing...or three."

Rebecca looked over, terrified at how drunk Darian suddenly sounded. His right side was covered in blood. She could see it trickling down his vest, dripping onto the growing wet spot on his pants. "Hoyt."

He glanced at her as she raised her shotgun to cover his side.

"Stop Hudson's bleeding. Locke, toss me your shotgun mags. I'm down to one and whatever I have left in this." She gestured at her Saiga, not letting the muzzle waver from where she needed to cover.

Before Locke could get her the magazines, Hoyt spoke up.

"Boss. Incoming." The dread in Hoyt's voice nearly strangled the tiny flits of emotions that were starting to break through her laser-focused survival instincts.

He wasn't looking at the trees, or even at anything on the island. Using a knife, he was cutting off the leg of his pants, presumably to create a makeshift bandage for Darian, but his eyes remained locked on the ocean.

Ready to face whatever was coming, Rebecca twisted to the side. There was a boat—too small to be carrying another army—cruising toward them. The hull was painted white, and it nearly glowed on the moonlit water. The noise from its engine had been covered by the blasts of gunfire until it was almost on them.

Unsure of the identity of the occupants, Rebecca stood and sidestepped to the water's edge, trying to move so she could see the approaching boat and the island full of shooters at the same time.

Exhausted and running low on ammo, she braced for what the boat's arrival might mean.

39

"I 'm guessing you're not getting off work anytime soon." Ryker's falsely chipper voice called out from the boat.

Rebecca was simultaneously surprised and mortified to see Ryker.

"What the hell! Ryker, shut up and get down." She gave Locke a hand as the boat drifted into the wash, helping her deputy hobble to the side.

"Well, that's a fine thank-you." Ryker leaned back, tilting the off-board motor out of the water, then stayed there, keeping the boat balanced as Locke had to sprawl across the gunwale to pull himself inside. His eyes widened at the sight of Locke's leg. "What the hell?"

Rebecca braced Locke's foot and gave him the final heave he needed to roll onto the bow.

Ryker's jovial attitude disappeared as he surveyed the shoreline. With a forced whisper, he called out to Rebecca. "State police caught the smugglers at the marina. I thought your night would be over, so I came to give you a ride home."

"Pretty good timing." Hoyt grunted, dragging Darian up out of the surf and toward the boat. The leg of his trousers was stuffed into the right armpit of Darian's vest, stemming some of the blood flow, but Darian's side was slick as Rebecca helped lift him into the boat.

That's not good.

Locke and Ryker couldn't help at all until they had Darian most of the way in or the small craft would flip over. It'd looked like a haven when Ryker'd pulled up, but now that they were struggling to get a third person aboard, she realized just how small the vessel was.

A two-seater was how he'd explained it to her. With Darian and Locke piled on top of each other in the front, it was already starting to dip low. As she grabbed the rim of the boat, she felt it drag against the sand.

"Dammit." Rebecca paused with ocean wavelets pushing at her knees, shoving her back toward shore. She took a deep, steadying breath. "Locke, give me those mags!" She had to lean forward to take them from him as he struggled to pull them from his belt. "Frost, turn the boat around. I'll cover."

Locke slapped the two full Saiga magazines into her hand.

She ignored his intense gaze as she slipped them into her empty pouches then turned and kept an eye on their back trail. "Can you call for backup, Ryker?"

"No reception."

That was what she'd been afraid of. All their communication methods were cut off. "They're jamming us. We've got to get out of here. Now." Rebecca heard a noise to her right, the same place she'd heard it before. "Frost, get on the boat."

Frost groaned as he dug into the soft sand and maneuvered the boat back into deeper water.

"You first, Boss." He wasn't close enough to actually touch her, but she saw him reach out.

"Don't fuck around, Frost. Get on that boat." She raised the shotgun to eye level, her voice dropping as she controlled her breathing and prepared to fire at the shadows shifting near the beach. "Your reach is almost a foot longer than mine. Now get your ass in that boat so you can haul me up after."

There was a long pause.

"Now."

She heard a splash as Hoyt pulled himself out of the water and into the boat.

Rebecca didn't see anything, but she knew someone was watching.

She pulled the trigger.

It sounded louder than normal and echoed strangely. So did the man's scream that followed. Almost like it had come from behind her.

There was a *thump* on the boat followed by a groan.

She turned, horror consuming her body.

Ryker was clutching at his chest, a stain of blood spreading from the middle out. He collapsed. His head cracked against the steering wheel. He didn't even try to brace himself as he fell the rest of the way, which told her he was unconscious. The boat tipped wildly as the men thrashed, trying to get behind cover in the front. More bullets flew out of the trees.

Rebecca whipped around to face the source.

Two shots were all she had before her shotgun was empty.

A man fell dead, breaking through the scraggly myrtle he'd tucked himself into. Before he hit the ground, she turned back to the boat.

Holes were punched through the side. It was already sitting low in the water with twice the number of passengers as intended. Thankfully, it was a small target, so it wasn't too perforated—only a few holes in the sides and none she could see in the hull.

Then she heard the gurgle. The stench of gasoline hit her nose. She raised her eyes and stared at the motor.

Clear liquid gurgled and trickled down the side. Their only chance of getting off the island was spilling out into the water.

Rebecca slung the strap of the shotgun sling onto the blades of the propeller. She yanked it down and the trickle of gas slowed.

She stared at the low-riding boat, the punctured engine, and the three men bleeding out on it. The harsh reality of their situation kicked in hard. The boat couldn't handle all of them and safely make it away from the island.

But I already knew that, didn't I? And I already know what I'm going to do...

Hoyt had a wife and two sons who loved him. A mother-in-law who invited him over for holiday dinners.

Darian had a family who loved him too. A wife and baby he'd been working so hard to get to spend time with on a sunny beach one day.

Locke, refusing to do what was demanded of him, proved he was just starting to turn his life around. He deserved a second chance, if nothing else. Looking at him now, knowing what she was about to sacrifice, she hoped she was right about him.

Ryker...his eyes were closed. He was still unconscious. That was a horrible sign.

"Hoyt, get everyone back to the island." Rebecca's breath hitched in her chest, but she ignored it. "And if you need, the paper files are in my spare bedroom stacked behind the bookcase."

"Why are you...?" His eyes widened and he tried to reach for her. There were too many wounded bodies in his way. "West, no!"

Rebecca shoved the boat with all her might, pushing it out into the current. "Go! That's an order."

"Rebecca! Damn you!"

"Sorry, Hoyt. Get them home."

"Sir!" Darian struggled to pull himself upright. His arm swung up in an arc. One more shotgun magazine plopped onto the beach behind her. "Stay alive!"

"Back at ya, Darian!" She hated to let him down, but she also didn't see how it was possible for her to survive on her own. As good as her training was, this island was filled with the enemy.

And every one of them knew where Rebecca was.

"No! Don't go playing Rambo, dammit!" Hoyt screamed obscenities as he pushed the throttle, and the propeller sprayed her with water.

"I was thinking Gandalf!" Rebecca caught herself right before she slipped off the ledge that formed the very edge of the tiny island. She'd gone as far as she could. The boat sped away, white paint shining in the moonlight making it an easy target.

And voices started calling out from behind her.

She had to stop them before they could take down the boat.

SLAMMING the rear door shut on the cruiser, Rhonda tapped the roof, signaling the trooper inside that he was good to go.

That was the last transport out. They'd managed to take down the three men who'd been lounging in the cabin of the *Clam Strips* with almost no effort. Realizing they were surrounded and outnumbered had gone a long way in her favor, she was sure. It might also have had something to do with the long history, and criminal records, all three of the men had in three different states.

The only thing missing was a full confession, but she was sure they'd get that soon enough. Right now, the three men were standing by their story that they'd salvaged a yacht they'd found adrift. When asked why they were at the marina, they claimed they'd looked up the legal owner and had tracked him there. They were hoping to get in contact with him to return it.

She didn't buy it. They didn't even know the name Landon Hannity. Just in case, she'd asked the curious marina members who had come over if he was a local. They said he was a member there. That was probably where they'd gotten their weak alibi.

A sudden thought occurred to Rhonda, and she glanced around. They'd been chattering on the radio for at least half an hour now, talking about the takedown, and she realized she hadn't heard Rebecca's voice yet.

"Has anyone called the sheriff?" She looked around at her men and only got headshakes and confused glances. Pulling the phone out of her pocket, she grinned. "Looks like I get to be the one to give her the good news, then."

Rebecca's phone rang, then immediately went to voicemail. Rhonda frowned and called the station instead. If anyone knew a better way to contact the sheriff, it would be Viviane.

40

The stink of engine oil burned her throat. Which, logically speaking, she knew wasn't possible. It had been gasoline that dribbled out, not oil. The smell was all in her head.

Rebecca stayed low on the shore, wavelets splashing her face as she pulled a magazine from her pouch and reloaded her shotgun once more. The reactive nausea washed away.

Voices of men kept getting closer.

Most of her was hidden behind a low dune. She held her elbow high, awkwardly bracing the shotgun against her bicep.

This was going to hurt like a bitch and might rip her shoulder out of its socket, holding it so poorly, but it was the only thing she could come up with for right now.

She'd been joking with Hoyt about playing Gandalf. But it'd been partially true. She could not let these men pass. Even letting them onto the beach and having enough time to aim was too much to allow.

They had to be stopped before they could shoot the boat

taking her men away. Her knowledge of boats was limited, but she couldn't imagine that it'd survive an additional hole.

The low dunes, she knew, provided the added benefit of acting as both camouflage and a minor shield. Sand could at least slow or turn a bullet.

Five men stepped out of the trees. In the faint moonlight, teeth flashed as they grinned, thinking they were about to corner their prey where there was no escape.

It gave her a bit of satisfaction to see there were plenty of bruises and bloody wounds among them.

The one in front, a stupidly grinning man with a chipped front tooth, shifted his eyes, and she knew he had to have seen the white boat in the distance.

As fast as she could, Rebecca pulled the trigger on her Saiga, emptying half the magazine. As she swung it left and right, her bones took a hammering and her forearms screamed in adrenaline-muted pain.

One man dropped immediately. Two more staggered.

She leaned forward and squeezed six more times. Staying upright was the best she could manage. The recoil pushed her back hard, spinning her slightly. Without her full body weight to keep her in place, her feet slid in the sand.

Still, it worked. Five bodies lay on the beach.

When she released the magazine, it floated away on the water.

Holding her gun aloft, she scrambled and rolled to the next dune.

She didn't know how many more bullets she'd need. Maybe one. Maybe another dozen. The trees had covered the cartel men's numbers.

Crouching low, she moved up to more solid ground but kept herself as low as possible. It was just her and an unknown number of enemies. All she had to do was survive, at least long enough for the boat to be out of range, and hopefully long enough for them to send her backup.

Keeping as low as possible, Rebecca moved for the magazine Darian had left for her in the sand. With that and Locke's last magazine in her belt, she had twenty-four shots left. That should be enough—if she ignored the fact that she'd already burned through almost a hundred rounds tonight. She went to load in her second magazine and—

A bullet tore through her bicep a split second before she heard the report. The shotgun fell from her grip as her arm spasmed in pain.

Out of instinct, Rebecca leapt to her left. She was still crouching and had all the strength in her legs, but the weight of the barrel dangling from her sling dragged at her.

"You dropped this." A tall man wearing a balaclava over his face walked out of the trees where he'd been crouched. He held her Ruger up, mocking her with it as he holstered his own. "Do you want it back?"

Rebecca rolled to her side. A flash of burning pain cramped up her arm as saltwater-soaked sand invaded the wound. Until the cramping stopped, her right arm was completely useless.

The screams of a dying man.

The stink of stale oil on concrete.

Her arm hanging useless as...

The masked man walked closer, pointing her own gun at her head. The shock and horror of her present situation was enough to yank her out of her PTSD flashback. This time, there was no cavalry coming. No one had her back.

She was alone.

But she knew one thing he didn't.

"Fuck you. Go ahead."

"Feisty. Don't worry. I'll make it quick." His eyes crinkled up at the sides as he grinned. "You know what? I take that back. Go ahead and worry. You've been messing up my operation all week. I'm going to take my time and enjoy this." He leaned over her, the gun barrel swinging down to point at her kneecap.

He pulled the trigger.

And nothing happened.

She'd unloaded the Ruger before losing it in the tumble of getting hit in the shoulder earlier.

"Sorry, but I don't think we've been properly introduced." Rebecca rocked to her right, pulling a canister of pepper spray from her pouch, and shot the spray in his face.

The evening breeze coming off the ocean at her back carried the aerosolized irritant, spreading it quickly and coating his head and face. He opened his mouth to let loose a scream that dissolved in a fit of coughing. He pawed at his eyes with the back of his glove.

Wrong move.

The oil-based spray soaked into the fabric of his gloves and mask, holding the irritant against his face no matter how much he thrashed. He tossed away the empty Ruger and pulled his own gun, aiming wildly.

Rebecca took that opportunity to get on her feet. She grabbed his wrist and twisted, forcing him to drop the gun. It landed in the shadows of the sand dunes, and she almost went for it.

But he recovered faster than she thought possible, yanking the balaclava off as he twisted around on one foot and kicked her in the middle of her chest. Some ribs broke under his boot with an audible *crunch*.

"I'm the person who's going to end you. But you can call me Wes, bitch."

The blow knocked Rebecca back. Her knees sagged with the pain, and she struggled to regain her breath.

Wes's face was burning red with rage, and a jagged white scar on his forehead stood out in stark contrast.

His fist was coming for her face.

Rebecca jerked back to dodge. Her ribs cramped brutally, and if she'd had any breath left in her body, it would've been squeezed out. She'd managed to escape direct impact, so the punch was only a glancing blow on her temple.

Still, it was enough to make her dizzy, then fill her body with agony as she crumpled and her broken ribs twisted with the movement. Pushing down the pain, Rebecca took a deep breath and jumped to her feet.

Any moment now, she'd get her third wind—another pulse of adrenaline that would help dull the pain and allow her to fight. She was sure of it.

His left fist came up and caught her in the jaw, smashing her teeth together. Blood filled her mouth.

Doing her best to turn with the punch, she brought her right leg up and scored a kick to his side. It was like kicking a tree, and the shock of the blow raced up her body.

She took a blow to her right inner thigh but refused to allow her breath to be knocked out of her again. Controlling her breath was the only way she could get through this.

Which would be a lot easier if she hadn't already spent the last hour fighting for her life. She was exhausted. Hell, she was miles beyond exhausted.

"Maybe I should take it a little easy on you."

Rebecca braced herself for some stupid sexist comment before he very obviously didn't take it easy on her.

"You and your men took down all fifteen of mine. Shit, that means I don't have to share my split with anyone else." He laughed, tears streaming down his face. Not for his fallen companions—it was only a chemical reaction caused by the pepper spray she'd coated him with, which he was already able to ignore. It might be harder for him to see through his tear-filled eyes, but it wasn't going to stop him.

He lashed out with a knife. She hit his wrist and twisted it, forcing him to drop the weapon—but not before he sliced her side open. The cut was followed by another punch to her face that washed away the new burning pain.

Rebecca spun away, stumbling backward. Even with the small, empty cannister of pepper spray clutched in her hand, she didn't think her fists were anywhere near as hard as his were. If his body was like striking a tree, his knuckles felt like stone against her cheekbones.

And he was too fast for her to dodge them. He pummeled her face, and with her right arm barely functional, she couldn't block or dodge most of his punches. All she could do was keep moving backward, lessening the force of the blows, and not allowing him to get a rhythm as she shifted sporadically. It slowed down the beating she was taking, but that was about all.

Then Wes stopped. And laughed.

Chills raced down her spine, wondering what else he could be planning to extend her painful death.

41

"**D**o you think I'm stupid?" Wes pointed at the ground and twisted away from her.

Rebecca didn't understand his question for a moment. Backing up again, she spit a mouthful of blood onto the sand between them.

"Did you really think I didn't notice you were moving toward that spare magazine this whole time?"

If he had, he was doing better than she was. While she was aware the mag was somewhere around this area, her cheeks were so swollen and her head spinning so badly that she wasn't certain of her location.

Rebecca struggled to come up with a plan, any plan. If she could just get some space between them...

The scarred man turned and walked away, just a few steps to her left, but it was enough...

He scooped up the shotgun magazine Darian had thrown. "This what you're trying to get to?"

Rebecca laughed, making her head spin horribly. She reached behind her with both hands, finally able to grab the shotgun dangling from its strap on her back, and swung it in front of her body, the barrel pointed at Wes.

He watched her with a smirk as she twisted the shotgun, showing the empty slot where the magazine should be, the bolt still locked open.

"You mean for this? Yeah, a shotgun isn't very useful without the ammo to go in it."

He opened his mouth—probably to laugh at her again—and she brought her right arm around, slammed Locke's last spare magazine into place and racked the bolt. In the same moment, she pulled the trigger.

Wes took the hit dead center. And the next four as well as she tilted the muzzle down to follow his falling body.

"No, I wasn't angling for that." Rebecca finally answered him with a smile as she walked forward.

His chest, stomach, legs, and throat were all perforated. Blood poured out of him like sauce from a strainer.

Looking down, she watched the light slowly dim from his eyes. Or maybe the light was dimming in hers. It was so hard to see now, even harder to think. "I was moving to get enough space to pull my gun, actually."

Too exhausted to keep standing, Rebecca fell to her knees. "Oh, and yes. I do think you're stupid."

The light kept getting dimmer, and Rebecca rolled her head over to stare at her arm. Blood was streaming out at a steady pace. A small voice in her mind reminded her that somewhere on this island there was a med kit she could use. And a bottle of water, at least. She was so thirsty, and everything hurt.

With a mighty struggle, she managed to lift her head, then her body, and look toward the trees. They seemed so far away.

Rebecca groaned. "Frost was right. Being Rambo sucks."

She took a shuffling step forward, then another, her left hand clutching her shotgun, and hoped stupid Wes had been right about at least one thing.

That he was the last man on the island. She couldn't take any more.

THE BRIGHT LIGHTS of the search and rescue helicopters swept over Little Quell Island. They were large enough to cover the whole island, so flashlights were barely needed.

Rhonda and the entire Marine police swept the sand and trees.

The drug runners never showed—probably took one look at all the action and turned tail.

Voices called out, one after another, as they found more corpses, discarded weapons, and piles of shells. Rhonda's heart stopped every time the officers announced they'd found another body.

An island this small shouldn't have been able to hide so many bodies or so many secrets. At the same time, she desperately hoped to hear another body call. Ten corpses in, and they still couldn't find the sheriff. The first body she'd seen had been blown apart by close shotgun fire.

That felt so long ago.

While the deputies and Ryker were all at the hospital being checked out, they still hadn't found Rebecca, not alive or dead. Every officer clearing the island was calling out nonstop for any remaining members of the crew that had attacked the sheriff's department to stand down and surrender. Surely, if Rebecca were still alive, she would've called back already. Was it possible they'd taken her instead of killing her?

That thought was worse than the idea of finding her dead.

As Rhonda searched, those same thoughts kept running through her mind. How had they gotten the drop on Rebecca and her men? Rhonda's team had found the jammers, so at least she knew why she hadn't heard from them and why they hadn't responded. Did someone leak their plans? On an island as small as Shadow, it was impossible to keep their movements completely hidden, but it didn't explain how the—

"I found her!"

Dr. Bailey Flynn was off like a flash, ignoring her promise to stay next to the special agent as she raced toward the call. And Justin Drake was on her heels, while Rhonda swerved through the scraggly trees, slipping on the wet leaves before stumbling to a halt.

Bailey was kneeling next to a body lying in a ring of shredded trees. A shotgun was propped on her left side with an empty water bottle beside it. Her right arm was wrapped in gauze around the bicep. The blood was fresh and trickled down the arm to drip off the elbow. Rhonda couldn't see much more with Bailey crouching over and hindering her view.

"Is she...?"

"She's alive. But not good." Bailey looked up and held her gloved hand out to take the bag Justin passed to her.

As she twisted to the side to open her bag, Rhonda finally got a look at Rebecca. The only way she knew it was her was because of the badge at her waist and the fact she had breasts. Her face was a mass of purple and black lumps.

"Justin, hold her in place so I can wrap this arm. She's bleeding too fast, but I haven't checked for neck injuries yet. Do you know what to do?"

"I know, Doc. No worries." Justin slid beside Rebecca,

kneeling on top of the shotgun like it wasn't there. He leaned forward, then paused and rocked back before he leaned forward again. "Doc, the blood's over here too."

"Shit!" Bailey looked up at Rhonda. "Tell your chopper to drop its board. We need to get her to a hospital, now!"

42

Angie Frost sat next to Rebecca's bed, her head propped up in her hands, her eyes swollen and puffy. A Bible was laid open in her lap where she'd been reading it. She was sleeping.

Rebecca had opened her eyes minutes back but didn't have the courage to wake her. The tear-swollen eyes told her everything she needed to know.

Someone on the boat—God, please let it only be one of them—had not survived.

One of her men was dead. For now, she didn't know who. For now, until Angie spoke, she could pretend it was none of them. Ignorance, in this case, was bliss. Angie was a rock, not just to Hoyt but to everyone in the department. If she'd been sobbing as hard as her face indicated, the news wasn't good.

Instead, Rebecca looked around the hospital room.

It was spacious, as far as such things went. There was enough room for at least two people to stand between the door and where the curtain around her bed would fall if it was pulled to give her privacy. The TV mounted in the upper corner of the room was turned off. She glanced at the whiteboard near the door. It was Thursday, August sixth.

As stiff and weak as she felt, she suddenly wished they had written the year on the board too. Had she been out for two days or a year and two days? Two years? That seemed weird.

With a wobbly neck, she managed to turn her head and saw what she expected. A metal box was connected to the IV pole next to her bed, dispensing strong painkillers. Morphine would explain the way her head was swimming and the strange path her thoughts had taken. Of course it hadn't been two years, just two days.

And yet, Angie looked like she had aged ten years.

Rebecca's heart wrenched, and it was hard to breathe. She pressed her lips together to hold in a sob. Trying to distract herself, she looked down.

There was a button in her right hand. The nurse had probably tucked it there after whatever surgery Rebecca had undergone. Setting that button down, she pulled out the neck of her gown and inspected her body.

Cuts and scrapes blended in with her purple-and-black torso. Broken ribs were always so ugly. A large bandage covered her left side, the white of it standing out starkly against the darker colors.

It was where she'd been cut with the knife.

That reminded her, and she pulled up the sleeve of her right arm. A bulky band of gauze was wrapped there too.

Rebecca remembered the burn, the bizarre twisting feeling. The arm becoming useless just when she needed it most. Maybe if she'd been able to use both arms, she could've saved herself some of the beating.

"No." Her words were thick and sticky, like her mouth.

It wouldn't have mattered how many arms she had. She'd been outmatched, pure and simple. Bigger, stronger, faster, with a longer reach. She'd done everything she could and had only managed to survive because he made a mistake. One simple mistake on his part had allowed her to reload and kill him before he killed her.

"Rebecca? Honey? Are you awake?"

Rebecca rolled her head over to find Angie staring at her.

"I'm awake." She looked down at the morphine button and debated using it. "How bad am I?"

"Pretty bad, dear." Angie closed her Bible and set it on one of those roller tables. "You've got four broken ribs, a broken cheek and eye socket, a bullet wound in your bicep, a broken bone in your foot, and a lot of stitches in your side." She leaned over and pressed the nurse call button on the bed. "Do you need anything?"

Are my men alive?

"Water, please."

Angie snatched up a cup sitting on Rebecca's bedside table. She held the cup close enough for Rebecca to take with her left hand.

Rebecca sucked down the water as fast as she could, clearing her mouth and throat. "Were we able to catch anyone?" She had to set the cup down as her hand and arm started to shake.

Angie slid the table closer so she didn't have to stretch. "No. No one on the island, at least. They were all dead. The investigation has been going on without you." Tears welled up in her eyes and she looked at Rebecca, choosing her next words carefully. "They had to put Ryker in a medically induced coma. He has a traumatic brain injury."

Rebecca's breath released in a gasp before Angie ploughed on. "There's something else you should know."

No. No. No.

"Who?"

"Rebecca, I—"

"Tell me who didn't make it."

Tears trickled down Angie's cheeks. "Darian."

Rebecca had to look away, turning her gaze to the ceiling tiles. They were the same, no matter where she went. White with irregular holes.

That was as far as she was willing to think right now. As far as she could. She was a coward. She knew it. And for right now, in this moment, she didn't care. Tears burned their way down her cheeks. "I only thought I knew what hurt felt like."

Nodding, Angie blotted at the tears burning Rebecca's swollen cheek.

Rebecca's chest was a scattered mess of cramps and nearly electric twinges that had nothing to do with her beating heart.

"Go ahead and push the button, honey. It will take the pain away."

That sounded like an amazing plan.

I'm so sorry, Darian. So sorry, Lilian. Mallory.

Rebecca pushed the button and let black, fluffy cotton take the pain away.

43

Rebecca walked through the cemetery, counting the rows. The markers stretched off into the horizon and disappeared over a slight hill. The atmosphere was as calm and tranquil as anyone could hope for. She spotted a few other visitors taking their own quiet paths. They all kept to themselves, showing a level of compassionate courtesy she desperately needed.

After a couple of weeks' worth of nightmares starring Wesley Garrett—gun runner, drug runner, and hired killer for the Amado Cartel—it was strange to be surrounded by so much serenity.

She'd woken up with her heart pounding, cold sweat pouring down her back, and muscles twitching for days on end. Now the heavy peace of Arlington National Cemetery settled around her.

For the moment, it appeared their firefight with organized crime had stopped both sides from running drugs or guns. Rhonda had run patrols along the probable boat lanes since that horrid night. No yachts were running dark. No one was out of place or suspicious. Though Rebecca had the sneaking suspicion this was a temporary lull, as long as the waters were silent and still for a little while, she would take it.

A cool breeze brushed against her hair, lifting tendrils away from her face. The fresh air revived her, soothing her wounds as she walked along row after row of names.

Once she was where she needed to be, she carefully knelt. She was certain that sitting on the ground would be impossible to get up from. This seemed more appropriate anyway.

"Sorry it took me so long to get here." She looked around again as a pair of cardinals started singing somewhere nearby. "I've never been to Arlington before. Lilian says you always thought it was peaceful. And when we learned you were eligible, because of that medal you never talked about, we knew this was where you belonged."

Rebecca ran her fingers over the name on the white headstone. *Corporal Darian Hudson. Beloved father, husband, friend, and hero.*

"You saved them. Did you know that?" Tears trickled down her cheeks again. She'd never been a crier before, but as she held out the little rattle she'd been asked to bring, she couldn't help herself. "It was your flare that got Ryker's attention. It was your idea to try the phones once you were far enough away. Did you know you were dying then?"

Her voice failed her, and she had to take a moment to pull in several deep breaths. Her ribs screamed and protested, and she sobbed before pressing her wrist against her lips. The little rattle clattered in her grip, and she had to close her eyes.

"Thank you, Darian. Thank you for saving them. Thank you for saving me. I would've bled to death if Rhonda hadn't found me in time." She laughed. "I would be dead now, maybe Locke, too, if you hadn't brought that med kit."

Grief ripped through her.

"I blamed myself for not using it on you. Until I learned what really happened. The bullet that went in through the side of your vest hit your lung. You were choking on your own blood the whole time. And you never even let on. You knew you were dying, didn't you?"

She swiped at her nose, and the rattle sounded again. She laughed.

"Lilian wanted you to have this."

She dug with her fingers at the soft earth around the base of the marker until she'd made a divot big enough, then she tucked the little plastic rattle against the marker.

"She said it was your favorite toy when you'd play with Mallory. But it broke that morning, before you came in for your shift. You had the broken piece in your pocket. That part is down there with you. But the main part," she had to pause to get her tears under control before she could finish speaking, "the main part will be up here now. Always connected and always apart."

She sat back, covering her face with her hands for a moment before wiping the tears away again.

"Thank you, Deputy Hudson. You saved us all. Rest now and know that we will all be watching over Lilian and Mallory. We'll make sure she knows what a hero her father was."

Unable to think of anything else to say, Rebecca knelt there and simply allowed herself to cry.

She didn't have to put on a brave face here and now. No one was watching. No one was depending on her to be strong.

So she rested on her knees and kept crying. Not loudly, not sobbing, just letting everything she'd been holding in roll out of her eyes and down her face.

Darian's final words echoed deep in her soul. *I have only the utmost respect for my superiors.* Superiors. She might have outranked him in title, but she could never equal his rank as a selfless human being. *I am proud to serve under her.*

"I'm not the badass you thought I was. I couldn't save you. I'm the one who's proud to have served with you."

And now Mallory would have to grow up without a dad. Lilian had lost her soulmate. All because Rebecca couldn't protect the people who got close to her.

By the time she'd finished unburdening her guilt, the sun had noticeably moved. She felt a bit lighter, but she doubted the hole in her heart would ever fully heal.

Gathering herself and looking one last time at the white headstone with the baby rattle tucked against it, Rebecca finally got to her feet and turned toward home.

The End
To be continued...

Thank you for reading.
All of the *Shadow Island Series* books can be found on Amazon.

ACKNOWLEDGMENTS

How does one properly thank everyone involved in taking a dream and making it a reality? Here goes.

In addition to our families, whose unending support provided the foundation for us to find the time and energy to put these thoughts on paper, we want to thank the editors who polished our words and made them shine.

Many thanks to our publisher for risking taking on two newbies and giving us the confidence to become bona fide authors.

More than anyone, we want to thank you, our readers, for sharing your most important asset, your time, with this book. We hope with all our hearts we made it worthwhile.

Much love,
Mary & Lori

ABOUT THE AUTHOR

Mary Stone

Mary Stone lives among the majestic Blue Ridge Mountains of East Tennessee with her two dogs, four cats, a couple of energetic boys, and a very patient husband.

As a young girl, she would go to bed every night, wondering what type of creature might be lurking underneath. It wasn't until she was older that she learned that the creatures she needed to most fear were human.

Today, she creates vivid stories with courageous, strong heroines and dastardly villains. She invites you to enter her world of serial killers, FBI agents but never damsels in distress. Her female characters can handle themselves, going toe-to-toe with any male character, protagonist or antagonist.

Discover more about Mary Stone on her website.
www.authormarystone.com

Lori Rhodes

As a tiny girl, from the moment Lori Rhodes first dipped her toe into the surf on a barrier island of Virginia, she was in love. When she grew up and learned all the deep, dark secrets and horrible acts people could commit against each other, she couldn't stop the stories from coming out of the other end of her pen. Somehow, her magical island and the darkness got mixed together and ended up in her first novel.

Now, she spends her days making sure the guests at her beach rental cottages are happy, and her nights dreaming up the characters who love her island as much as she does.

Connect with Mary Online

facebook.com/authormarystone

twitter.com/MaryStoneAuthor

goodreads.com/AuthorMaryStone

bookbub.com/profile/3378576590

pinterest.com/MaryStoneAuthor

instagram.com/marystoneauthor

tiktok.com/@authormarystone

Made in the USA
Monee, IL
10 August 2023